COME FIND ME

(A Caitlin Dare FBI Suspense Thriller—Book 2)

Molly Black

Molly Black

Bestselling author Molly Black is author of the MAYA GRAY FBI suspense thriller series, comprising nine books (and counting); of the RYLIE WOLF FBI suspense thriller series, comprising six books; of the TAYLOR SAGE FBI suspense thriller series, comprising eight books; of the KATIE WINTER FBI suspense thriller series, comprising eleven books (and counting); of the RUBY HUNTER FBI suspense thriller series, comprising five books (and counting); of the CAITLIN DARE FBI suspense thriller series, comprising five books (and counting); and of the REESE LINK mystery series, comprising five books (and counting).

An avid reader and lifelong fan of the mystery and thriller genres, Molly loves to hear from you, so please feel free to visit www.mollyblackauthor.com to learn more and stay in touch.

ISBN: 978-1-0943-3103-4

BOOKS BY MOLLY BLACK

MAYA GRAY MYSTERY SERIES
GIRL ONE: MURDER (Book #1)
GIRL TWO: TAKEN (Book #2)
GIRL THREE: TRAPPED (Book #3)
GIRL FOUR: LURED (Book #4)
GIRL FIVE: BOUND (Book #5)
GIRL SIX: FORSAKEN (Book #6)
GIRL SEVEN: CRAVED (Book #7)
GIRL EIGHT: HUNTED (Book #8)
GIRL NINE: GONE (Book #9)

RYLIE WOLF FBI SUSPENSE THRILLER
FOUND YOU (Book #1)
CAUGHT YOU (Book #2)
SEE YOU (Book #3)
WANT YOU (Book #4)
TAKE YOU (Book #5)
DARE YOU (Book #6)

TAYLOR SAGE FBI SUSPENSE THRILLER
DON'T LOOK (Book #1)
DON'T BREATHE (Book #2)
DON'T RUN (Book #3)
DON'T FLINCH (Book #4)
DON'T REMEMBER (Book #5)
DON'T TELL (Book #6)

KATIE WINTER FBI SUSPENSE THRILLER
SAVE ME (Book #1)
REACH ME (Book #2)
HIDE ME (Book #3)
BELIEVE ME (Book #4)
HELP ME (Book #5)

FORGET ME (Book #6)
HOLD ME (Book #7)
PROTECT ME (Book #8)
REMEMBER ME (Book #9)
CATCH ME (Book #10)
WATCH ME (Book #11)

RUBY HUNTER FBI SUSPENSE THRILLER

IF I RUN (Book #1)
IF I TELL (Book #2)
IF I LIVE (Book #3)
IF I FORGET (Book #4)
IF I RETURN (Book #5)

CAITLIN DARE FBI SUSPENSE THRILLER

COME GET ME (Book #1)
COME FIND ME (Book #2)
COME TAKE ME (Book #3)
COME CATCH ME (Book #4)
COME SAVE ME (Book #5)

REESE LINK MYSTERY

BEYOND REASON (Book #1)
BEYOND REACH (Book #2)
BEYOND REPAIR (Book #3)
BEYOND DOUBT (Book #4)
BEYOND NORMAL (Book #5)

PROLOGUE

There was a hazard ahead, a potential danger lurking. Now, he had to search it out.

Carl Naylor narrowed his eyes, peering through the onslaught of icy rain at the tracks stretching out before him. There had been reports of vandalism from this section of rail, in this remote part of northern Ohio, one of the areas where a complexity of old and new rail lines connected. An incoming driver had called it in.

By the time the message had reached Carl, it had been garbled, and the driver's phone was off. So, all he knew was that there was something wrong, somewhere, within this section of train track near the junction.

Carl had set out into a late fall rainstorm to do a safety inspection.

"Most likely just a loose jointbar," he muttered to himself through numb lips, as he trudged along the tracks, ducking his head to avoid a gust of the icy rain.

The new tracks in this section had all been joined together with the old, a few years back now, using the metal jointbars. It was his opinion that someone had done a shoddy job. There were a few of them that had worked loose in the past few months.

"Safety risks," he muttered, wishing someone else had been on duty this particular morning. This weather was vile. Carl had finally gotten around to having a haircut, two months overdue, and now he was regretting that his thick, dark hair was no longer curling over his neck and his ears, which felt exposed, and freezing, even under his waterproof hat.

But storm or no storm, long hair or short, he couldn't ignore any safety risk that might interfere with the running of the trains. And although vandalism was unlikely in this remote, rural part of the world, Carl's favorite expression was never say never.

There were psychos out there who would take glee in destroying a section of track and watching as the train veered off it. That, he knew. Folks were strange. In his opinion, you should expect the worst from humanity.

Carl was in no mood to deal with anyone who might wish to cause trouble on the line. He'd just come off a long night shift, and he was cold and wet and tired. This inspection should have been done by the rail engineer working the day shift, but the rail engineer working the day shift had called in sick with bronchitis.

Since this was urgent, it was now into the overtime hours for him.

All he wanted to do was to get back to the warmth of the station, to dry out after his inspection of the line, and then head home.

He walked along the tracks, bending down to inspect the jointbars, shining the light on them, testing them for any signs of a misalignment or looseness.

There!

He bent down, his gloved hand tugging at the metal bar. It was very loose, he could see it was askew and feel it move, and the movement of the train along the tracks would work it still looser. Luckily, it was a quick repair job, nothing more than the tightening of the bolts. Getting them really tight. As in, immovable.

He got the hammer and wrench out of his backpack and set to work, spraying the jointbar with oil before inserting that hammer and wrench into place, and then screwing the bolt as tight as it would go. He stamped down on the wrench with his booted foot, feeling the metal squeak in protest as he slammed it tighter still.

There. It had been a long walk for a small job.

He straightened up, shivering. His back was stiff, and his legs were aching as he squinted his eyes against the wind and the sleet. It occurred to Carl suddenly that maybe the walk wasn't over yet.

He had found a necessary repair, but now he was asking himself the uneasy question: how had anyone seen this? Unless you were walking along the actual track, that loose jointbar was almost invisible. A driver passing by on the parallel track would have had to have been very lucky to have spotted it. So, maybe this hadn't been the reason for the report, and there was something else. Farther on.

Carl sighed. Now that he'd had the thought, it wouldn't leave his mind. It couldn't hurt to look a little farther. After all, he was already freezing, even through his waterproof coat, because the wind was blowing the rain through the gaps in the collar and sleeves. It wasn't like he could get colder or wetter. So, he might as well push on.

Hunching his shoulders, feeling grumpy that he'd had the thought and earned himself still more time out in the bad weather, he trudged along the track, keeping a lookout to the left and right for obstacles near the rails, as well as ahead.

Blinking water out of his eyes, he thought he saw something. A few steps later, he was sure of it. Someone had dumped a bundle of rags on the track. And of course, people being what they were, there was no guarantee there wasn't something wrapped up inside them—a metal bar, or maybe even worse.

People. He didn't trust them. Not after nearly twenty years of working on the railways.

Carl knew there was a good chance that someone had dropped the bundle of rags along the track, and they'd just been careless. But what if they weren't? What if this was a deliberate attempt to sabotage the train?

He walked up to the pile of rags, sodden and sad looking. Lifting his booted foot, he gave it an experimental push, to test what it might be.

Then his eyes widened as he felt the odd solidity of the bundle within, the strangely disturbing feel of it. As if he'd touched something he shouldn't. Something that had a give to it, not a metallic jangle. But it wasn't solid like a sandbag.

This was not what he'd expected. What on earth was inside here?

He reached out a gloved hand and tugged at a corner of the rags.

And then, Carl yelled aloud.

The ragged edge unfurled, and it exposed a tangle of dark hair that streamed out, wet and tumbled, like old, blackened weeds. And beyond that, the sheet white of a woman's face, with wide, staring eyes.

"No!" Dropping the sheet, Carl backed away.

This was a body. And, wrapped in those sheets, his frenzied mind told him that it couldn't have been killed by the train, there was no sign of that, this poor woman must have been killed elsewhere and dumped here.

He gasped in a breath, looking around him at the gray, rainy landscape that seemed suddenly full of threat. In this remote and isolated place, a murderer was at large.

CHAPTER ONE

Caitlin Dare stood outside the home's freshly painted front door. She took a deep breath, lifted the brass knocker, and brought it down with a bang.

This felt like a pivotal moment in her life. Nerves surged in her as she waited for the door to be answered.

She might be a seasoned FBI agent, with ten years of law enforcement experience under her belt, but this confrontation felt scarier than any takedown she'd done with her SWAT team. For so long, she had wanted to gather the courage to do this. At last, after all the uncertainty and holding back, she was ready to demand answers.

She lifted a hand and smoothed back her auburn hair, which was whipping against her face in the afternoon breeze. Her fingers felt cold, and not just from the weather.

This was bringing all her old demons raging. Anger, fear, and the desire for payback roiled inside her.

She heard footsteps approaching and tensed. A moment later, the door opened. Caitlin found herself staring at Uncle Josh.

The liar. The abductor, as she had thought of him with fear and anger ever since her sister's disappearance.

He'd lived well in the past decade since she'd last seen him. That was her first, shocked impression. His face was round, fleshy. His body heavier. He wore a shapeless, gray sweater and old jeans. Those ice blue eyes—the identical color to her own—were filled with surprise as he stared at her.

At least it made a change from that oddly intense, creepy expression that she remembered.

"Caitlin?" he said in a gravelly voice. "What are you doing here?"

She squared her shoulders, ready to take him on. "I'm here for answers," she said.

"Answers about what?" he shot back, although she was sure he knew.

"About Ella's disappearance. I want to know what happened, ten years ago, when she got on that train."

She saw his gaze slide sideways for just a moment before returning to her again. "Caitlin, I have no idea what happened to your younger sister! I was not working on that train. We discussed this. My shift ended four hours previously."

She'd expected him to dodge and dive. "You could have been there. Maybe not working as a conductor, but traveling as a staff member, as you were allowed to do."

"How many times do I have to tell you that I was nowhere near there?" He sounded smug, as if he was repeating a story that had already been believed and would be again. "I was not on that train, neither for my conductor's shift nor for travel. Sure, the police asked me, as you know. And as you know, that's what I said!"

"Why should I believe you?" Caitlin felt an odd kind of calm, as if she was somehow outside herself and watching this exchange. He might be answering reasonably now, but she felt as if by pressuring him, she was lighting a fuse, and soon she would see if it exploded.

"Are you saying you're better than the police? Smarter than they are?" It felt as if he was taunting her now.

"Maybe I know you better than they do," she said and saw his face darken.

"You have a completely false impression of me. Your accusations are so wild, I would even go so far as to say you're delusional." Now, his tone was insulting.

He moved to close the door. Caitlin shot out a hand and pushed it back open again. "Just one more question, please. Where were you, then? Do you have an alibi? Can you account for your time?"

If she could force him to crack, if he revealed he had been on that train, then she was going to get the case reopened. And then, maybe, Caitlin could discover the truth.

"I was at home in San Francisco. And your sister's disappearance is long over and done with. Leave me be now. You can't make it right." He was glaring at her now, but his words were as smooth as ever.

"Can you prove where you were?" she pressured.

"I'm not telling you that. It's not your business."

"I think it is my business," she said, her voice rising. "Because I think you know something."

Caitlin stared at him. It looked as if he was trying to control himself, but the fury was boiling inside him, threatening to explode.

"You don't know what you're talking about," he insisted.

"I'm going to find out what happened to my sister," she said. "I'm going to find out the truth."

"The truth? You've had the truth, girl!" he spat at her. "I'm not a liar like you!"

"What?" Caitlin was so shocked by his words that she took a step back. "A liar? What are you talking about?"

"You're a liar. You're obsessed with the fact that I might have been involved with this, and you've invented stories to prove it. What you don't see is that they are crazy, delusional. You're only destroying yourself by pursuing this. The family all think you're the troublemaker. They know what you're like because I've made sure to tell them." He sounded more self-satisfied than ever. "However, it's becoming tiresome now. You might be family, but don't think I haven't considered getting my lawyer involved in this, because I do have a right to privacy. And to not having people like you arrive on my doorstep to dredge up the past."

Now, he looked angry, but Caitlin saw defensiveness there too.

"You know something more. I'm sure of it," she insisted. "Why not just tell me? Whatever it is?"

"You want the truth? Here it is. Your sister vanished on that train. She was never seen again. Not a single trace of her was ever found. I told the police that."

"That's untrue! They found a scrap of fabric that was from her top. And it had a streak of blood on it. So, they did find something!"

He grabbed her arm now. His fingers dug into her flesh. "I was not on that train. I did not even see your sister on that day. You're living in a fantasy world. You've always been like this, inventing stories to make yourself feel better, to make things come out the way you want. Maybe you should know your place in the world and leave these matters alone."

He shook her arm.

Caitlin pulled away, shocked. His grip was unexpectedly strong, but so were his words. With a chill, she saw the hatred in his eyes. She was a threat to him. But he was going to keep defending himself against the threat. He was stonewalling her, and she couldn't break through. It felt as if she'd faced down her worst fears by arriving at his doorstep, but she knew the fight wasn't over.

"I have nothing more to say," said Uncle Josh. "You want me punished? You want to take me down? You want to see me in jail? Well, I'm not going to be jailed because of you! You're going to leave me be! You're going to leave me alone! You're going to stay away from me and my family!"

"It's my family too. My sister," she insisted, standing her ground. But Uncle Josh was continuing his tirade, so loudly that a passerby on the street turned and stared.

"You decided that I was a suspect. You created a story in your own head that I was the one who had your sister killed, and you decided that you were going to make me pay. Well, I'm going to make you pay!"

He jabbed a finger at her.

She'd never expected Uncle Josh to be so vindictive. She had expected to see guilt in his eyes, but all she could see was a desire for payback that was unsettling in its intensity.

"What do you mean, you'll make me pay?" she asked, suspicions flaring.

"I mean I'll take legal action. I'll get the courts involved, if that what it takes." He stepped forward, his voice filled with threat. "Who do you think you are? Do you think you're a saint? Do you think you're some kind of superhero? You have no proof of any misdoings. There is no proof, and I will not be persecuted by a member of my own family! My reputation is important to me, and you're trying to tarnish it."

He was advancing toward her, his face twisted with anger.

Caitlin backed away. It was time to go. She hadn't gotten through to him, and he hadn't broken or wavered from his story. But she was certain, now, that there was more. He knew more, even if he hadn't done more. The smugness in his tone, and that threat, were telling her so. Now she knew why this unsolved mystery had been gnawing at her mind for so many years.

"I'm leaving now," she said. "But I promise you that I will find the truth about what happened to Ella."

She turned and walked away, feeling disappointed, but also resolute. If it hadn't been him, then he was protecting someone else. That was now the possibility that was occurring to her after this confrontation.

And if so, did it mean that the person who really took Ella was now free and clear, protected by the passage of time and the fact that nobody had ever guessed at his identity?

She needed to take another look at what had happened, because there were too many secrets and not enough answers. If he wouldn't give them to her, then she was going to go out and find them.

CHAPTER TWO

Caitlin strode through the misty rain, following the walkway that led through the park. Just a week after the confrontation with Uncle Josh, she was on an important mission, and it had a strict time limit attached.

This was the first time she'd taken the neighbor's Jack Russell for a walk, after meeting them in the elevator of her new apartment block in Kansas City while she was moving in. The elderly woman had complained about her hip, and that walking her middle-aged, but energetic, dog wasn't as easy as it had been.

Caitlin had immediately offered to help out. Now, in the faint light of early morning, she and Charlie were out for a brisk, refreshing walk. They'd been around the park opposite her apartment, stopping a few times for Charlie to sniff out interesting smells and lift his leg against a tree trunk. Now, they were heading back, trying to outpace the light rain that was starting to fall.

Charlie's tail hadn't stopped wagging the entire way. This walk was clearly the best treat for him, and she felt the same way. She hadn't stopped grinning, either. He was the cutest dog, and she was pleased to have made her first four-legged friend in her new hometown.

Ever since facing up to Uncle Josh, his words had simmered at the back of her mind, impossible to erase. Now, out in this misty, fresh morning, she'd finally been able to put them aside for a while.

"We've had a great time, haven't we, Charlie? You were very good on the leash. And you'd better get used to this, because we're doing it again, at least twice a week from now on. You got yourself a new walking date, little guy!"

Charlie looked up at her, his tail wagging even harder as they headed into the lobby and over to the elevators.

Caitlin's new place was a third-floor, loft-style apartment on the outskirts of town. Modern and sleek, but in a more suburban location, it looked and felt a world away from the place she'd had in Atlanta when she'd worked for the FBI SWAT team.

And her new job was different too. Heading up a specialized railway crime unit that worked countrywide was a very different role from having been a member of the Atlanta-based team that had seldom worked outside the city and never outside the state. At first, she'd thought of this move as a demotion, but she'd since realized it was an opportunity to escape a work environment that had become increasingly toxic. And it was a job filled with potential—one that she could make her own.

She rode up with Charlie and then headed to the next-door apartment and tapped on the door.

"Shirley? We're back!" she called.

The door was opened, and the gray-haired woman took the leash from Caitlin with a smile.

"Oh, look how happy he is! You can see how bright his eyes are. Thank you."

"We both had a great time," Caitlin said, smiling back.

"Do you want to come in for coffee?"

She checked her watch. "I'd love to, another time. I'm on my way to meet my boyfriend now. His flight should have landed. But thank you for the offer."

"Next time," Shirley said. "Have a good day."

"You too." Turning away, thinking of her upcoming breakfast date, Caitlin felt a shiver of excitement. Having Mike promise to join her was the most unexpected, surprising, and wonderful part of this entire relocation. And this morning, he was coming here to explore job opportunities.

After breakfast, he would spend the day going to interviews and visiting a few of the local schools—as a math and science teacher, who also taught PE part-time, he wouldn't have difficulty finding the perfect position, she hoped.

The plan was that he would rent his own apartment for a while and settle in. Then, she hoped, they might live together.

She felt a flush of excitement at the thought of them being near each other, sharing their lives, and sharing a future.

Feeling full of enthusiasm about what this would bring, she hurried back to the elevator. Especially after the disastrous visit with Uncle Josh last week, Caitlin was looking forward to this positive move.

Walking across the road again, she headed for the breakfast spot where they'd agreed to meet after his early morning flight landed from Atlanta.

She didn't know the city well yet, so she'd chosen the cafe in the small shopping center across the park, hoping it was a place he'd like.

Plus, as a bonus, she could walk there. On her own and without Charlie, it took just ten minutes, and as she arrived, Mike was pulling up in his rental car.

"Hello!" she greeted him, feeling relieved that he was here at last. This "long distance" relationship they'd had since she'd made the move here had been more challenging than she'd expected. For some reason, she'd felt there was a distance between them, wider than just the extra miles that separated them.

The tall, dark-haired man, with a slightly retro, long, fringed haircut and wearing his school's branded tracksuit top, looked far too handsome to be a schoolteacher. He smiled at her, his green eyes warm, holding out a hand to draw her close.

"Hello!" he greeted her and gave her a kiss. "Lovely part of the world," he said, staring around as they walked in.

Caitlin felt cheered that he liked it. She felt surprisingly anxious about his opinion, and as if she was rooting for the area! It was a great sign that his first impressions were good.

Perhaps her anxiety was about more than just the new place, she acknowledged. She'd always wondered if Mike was serious about the relationship, or just happy to date her occasionally. So, really, it was his commitment that she was nervous about.

The waitress brought menus, and they ordered coffee and two breakfasts—eggs and bacon for him, grilled cheese for her.

The coffee shop was playing Lady Gaga on the radio. That had to be a good sign, Caitlin thought. That had been Ella's favorite music, and she'd been so used to hearing it from her sister's bedroom that the songs were now indelibly associated with Ella's memory, and she always found the music comforting.

"There are a few good schools close to here," she said. Although she'd already emailed him all the leads she could find, she felt as if she wanted to sell him on the possibilities. "When I've been driving around, I've seen a couple of bigger schools, a few remedial schools, and I've seen two private schools. So, lots of opportunities."

"Have you settled in well?" he asked.

"It's early days," she admitted. "But we've found a small office, a couple of miles from here, and we've hired a central controller who can coordinate things."

"Is that so?" he asked. “What’s she like?”

"She's an ex-policewoman who lives locally. She’s enthusiastic to be part of the unit and seems very competent. Hopefully, over time, we'll grow the unit further. We're looking at getting a second pair of investigators on board so that we can respond quickly to any crisis. I had no idea that there were so many railway crimes."

In her new role, Caitlin had been partnered up with Nathan Bridges, a railway special agent.

Caitlin still had no idea how the partnership with this railway cop was going to work out long term. They'd started off resenting each other. But their relationship had improved, slightly, as they'd worked together to solve their first serial murder case.

The task force was now a permanent fixture. She and Nathan had both gotten places here, in Kansas City, as it was a central point within the country.

"But what I don't understand is why you had to move here at all," Mike said, frowning.

"We need to be somewhere central," she said, feeling put out, because she was sure she'd told him that already. "The idea is that we'll be in the middle of the country, making it easier for us to cover the whole of the country."

"But why leave Atlanta? I thought you were doing so well in your job," he said. “I’m surprised you chose to relocate here, to be honest, Caitlin.”

Caitlin stared at him, temporarily at a loss for words. She wasn't sure what to say. She had thought Mike was excited about her new role, and not full of doubts. And it wasn’t like she’d had a choice. She'd been forced out of the SWAT team, unfairly. Her boss, Hume, and ex-partner, Fitch, had blamed it on the fact that she took rogue action and wasn't a good team player.

Rogue action that saved lives?

Ever since the FBI Academy days, where she'd been known as Rebel Dare for her propensity to act in the moment to solve a situation or get a fellow trainee out of danger, Caitlin knew her bosses had labeled her as hotheaded. But she'd always thought that her effective performance, her high takedown rate, had balanced out that trait.

It seemed not. She'd felt crushed when her trusted team had conspired to force her out and replace her. Hume had put her forward for the new task force specializing in railway crimes.

Now, Caitlin was realizing that her new opportunity gave her all the chances she needed to use her initiative, without the environment of the SWAT team that she now realized, in hindsight, had become increasingly oppressive.

She still didn't know if she was going to take things further, though, as she'd been unfairly treated, and she wanted to set the record straight. Her heart told her she should, but how could she do such a thing when she would be going head-to-head with a senior FBI employee with an impeccable record? It seemed impossible, but Caitlin had never been one to step away from a fight when it involved justice.

"I wasn't given a choice," she said to Mike.

"No?" he responded, eyebrows raised. “You had a good life there. I admired how you did your job, and also how you gave back—the extra self-defense classes you held after hours for people who needed them, the time you spent coaching kids on safety at the schools. You were part of the community.”

His words seared her. For a while, she had felt part of the community, but every FBI agent knew that they had to be moved where needed. This move had not been for positive reasons, or even legitimate reasons in her view, but it didn’t alter the fact that she had to be prepared for such a thing.

"They needed someone for this position, I was the best fit, and that's the way things work in law enforcement," she said firmly. “FBI agents relocate regularly. Being part of the railway task force is giving me the best chance I’ll have at permanence, here.”

She wasn't going to let him get under her skin or undermine her belief in her new role. She had no idea why he was even trying. Why wasn't he supporting her? Was he having second thoughts about the move, she wondered, feeling uneasy.

Their food arrived, and Caitlin dug in.

"What's your plan for today?" she asked.

"I'm going to go and meet with a couple of teachers at Westwood High," he said.

The high school was one of the larger schools in her new area, and having done some swift online research, she knew it had a strong academic reputation. Working there would be a step up in his career.

“Is it an actual job interview?” she asked. “Or just fact finding and making connections?”

"I'm only looking," he said, shrugging. "I'm not sure the school will be the right fit for me."

"It's a great school," she said.

He wasn't sounding as enthusiastic as she'd hoped he would.

"What about later?" she said. "I'm going to go into the railway task force offices after this. There's still a lot of setting up to do there, but if there's no emergency, I should be home by about five. We could have dinner somewhere. And will you be staying over?"

She assumed he would and was looking forward to the evening. But to her consternation, he shook his head.

"I have an evening function back home, so I'll be flying back at four."

"Oh," she said, suddenly deflated. She'd been looking forward to some quality time with him and to exploring the city with him. But why had he booked this function? Was he having second thoughts? She knew, though, that the school he worked for had a lot of after-hours activities, so presumably he’d been roped into one of those.

“I'll hopefully be able to come here again next month," he said.

Caitlin wolfed down her grilled cheese. Never mind the calories. Right now, she needed the comfort of it. This wasn't feeling right, or the way she'd wanted it to be. Having said he’d move, he now didn’t seem to be committing to anything—the new job, or the new area.

"Is everything okay?" she asked, reminding herself that this was a big change for him. It could not be easy or without its stresses.

"Everything's fine," he told her reassuringly, but she didn't believe it.

Then her phone rang. "I must take this," she said, seeing it was Aniyah, their new, ex-policewoman, office coordinator. Quickly, Caitlin picked up.

"Caitlin. Good morning," Aniyah said.

"Good morning," she responded, wondering what was up, because Aniyah sounded stressed.

"There's a new case called in. Murder. Can you get here as soon as possible? I'll need to organize for you and Nathan to fly out of state."

Adrenaline surged inside her. "I'll be there in ten minutes," she said.

She crammed the last of her grilled cheese into her mouth and downed her coffee. "Work emergency," she said to Mike, who nodded. "I'll be in touch later."

They kissed a quick goodbye, but as Caitlin left, she realized that she'd never thought her emotion on leaving their breakfast would be relief. Something was wrong; something was off kilter.

But there wasn't time to discuss it. The relationship trouble would have to take a back seat for a few hours, because she needed to focus all her attention on the serious case ahead.

CHAPTER THREE

Caitlin arrived at the railway task force's new HQ half an hour later. She felt expectant, nervous, and as if everything was at stake. She'd gone past her apartment to pick up her laptop bag and a change of clothes, and had then rushed straight to the small, third-floor office in a building two miles from her apartment.

This was their first murder case since the unit had moved to its new premises. What was this case about? And where was it? It could be anywhere. Which state was affected? What did the crimes involve?

Questions surged in her mind. Already, the pressure was on.

As soon as she walked into the one-room office, she saw Aniyah. The dark-haired, dark-eyed woman with a short, chic haircut and gold earrings was managing to juggle two phone calls, about seven different messages, and simultaneously answer emails and keep an eye on the news channel.

Caitlin felt excited to be working with their super-efficient, new administrator, who had eagerly transferred from being a police officer to her new role in the railway unit's admin office.

"Hello, Caitlin," she said.

"Morning, Aniyah."

"Nathan's on his way. He should be here any time now," she said, pushing up the sleeves of her red blouse and glancing again at the incoming messages on her computer.

In that case, Caitlin decided, the talk about the case could wait a minute so that Aniyah didn't have to repeat everything twice.

"How's Keisha doing?" she asked, taking a seat at the small desk in the corner.

Aniyah was a single mom to a five-year-old girl who'd recently started at a new kindergarten. Small talk didn't come easily to Caitlin, but she was determined that the relationships in this unit were going to be friendly and open. No backstabbing and no manipulation, she had resolved, thinking bitterly of her ex-unit.

"She's loving school. Already made friends. I can't believe how sociable she is," Aniyah admitted, glancing at the photo of the young girl she kept on her desk. Then it was her turn to ask the social question.

"Is your boyfriend arriving today?" Yesterday, Caitlin had mentioned this to Aniyah. "I hope it won't interfere with his time here, having this case to deal with," she added, frowning.

Caitlin frowned too. "No, it won't, because he has to fly back home this afternoon. I'm not sure why. Some evening function."

"That's a pity," Aniyah sympathized. "Still, I'm sure it'll be easier when he has a new job and is here full-time."

"I hope so," Caitlin said, but she couldn't help feeling filled with doubts when she thought about Mike. It didn't seem that things were working out the way she'd expected them to.

"Change is scary," Aniyah reassured her. "Maybe it's that. Maybe he's hesitant about the new start and the move."

"I guess that must be it," Caitlin agreed.

And then, Nathan walked in. "Morning, Caitlin. Morning, Aniyah. What's up with this new case?" he asked.

His tall, gangly frame and his blond, surfer boy looks were at odds with the smart, black railway police uniform he wore.

Caitlin still didn't know how the working relationship with Nathan was going to pan out. They had worked together well on their first case—eventually and after a very rocky start. But apart from those moments where they'd been a team when the chips were down, Caitlin was still dubious.

It seemed like they disagreed on everything else. Everything! They hadn't reached agreement on one single issue outside of that, without what felt like hours of conflict resolution. Even deciding how to lay out the office desks had nearly caused a full-on fight. As far as pictures on the wall went, it was fairly predictable that she'd gone straight for the mountain prints, loving the imposing strength of them, while Nathan had his heart set on the seascapes. Aniyah, in the end, had decided they'd take one of each. Conflict had been resolved—for that moment.

Their personalities were opposites. Nathan was more prudent—apart from the occasional moment of impulsiveness—and she was always ready to find a quicker way and was up for breaking rules if it meant saving lives.

But there was no time to worry about their differences now. Hopefully, with a case now on board and both of them focused on the bigger picture, they'd be able to handle themselves in a cooperative way. Caitlin had no illusions that their unit was still under scrutiny. The powers that were didn't let new units start up without monitoring them for years.

They could still be closed down a month from now, and that fear simmered at the back of her mind as they pulled their chairs around the small conference table. This office was still so new that it smelled of fresh paint and cleaning products.

It might be a small office, but to Caitlin, this felt like an important and auspicious fresh start. She shouldn't let fear rule her. Firmly, she told herself she could not allow the decisions of prejudiced FBI agents to affect her approach to work in her new role.

This new opportunity had made her realize that she didn't want to give up on her dream of being a successful law enforcement officer and fighting crime wherever she could, which had felt like it was in jeopardy.

But for now, every case counted, and she knew that every outcome would be carefully analyzed. Were they performing adequately? Was this crime fighting unit worth the investment? Was the team contributing to a better, safer environment for the difficult to police network of railways?

All those questions would be asked. She hoped their performance would provide satisfactory answers.

Aniyah clicked the mouse to activate her laptop screen again. "In the space of two days, two bodies have been found on train tracks in northern Ohio." They both stared at her intently as she turned the screen and pulled up a map of the state, pointing to the locations.

"They're within a ten-mile radius of this small town, Clearwell," she continued. "One body was found yesterday evening on a section of disused track near the main tracks. It was a couple of days old. Then early this morning, as they called that one in, the second body was found. Local police have asked for help as they suspect it's a serial."

Caitlin's eyes widened. "So, it sounds like these victims were not killed while on the tracks? If one set of tracks was disused?"

That had been her first impression—that the victims had been dumped while alive and died on the tracks. Horrific as that was, the other scenario, that they had been killed elsewhere and then moved, was even more perturbing.

Because it indicated a more twisted motive, Caitlin thought, with a shiver.

"I'm still waiting to clarify that this is the case for both victims," Aniyah said. "But so far, according to these notes, the coroner believes the second victim was killed elsewhere and then dumped."

"And the victims? Any ID as yet?" Nathan asked.

"No. One is a woman in her thirties, another is a woman in her twenties. They're working on ID and matching it up to missing persons reports as we speak," Aniyah said. "Both victims were wrapped in sacking and rags before being placed on the tracks."

The similarities in the modus operandi were sounding like a serial murderer at work, and Caitlin felt a chill.

"The second site is still an open crime scene." Aniyah was tapping more keys on her computer. "I'm going to be able to charter a flight to get you to the local airport at Clearwell, so you can head there straight away. I can organize for police to meet you on the other side."

She sounded excited. This was her first time setting these logistics up. Caitlin was impressed again by her calmness and efficiency. She could see how keen she was to prove herself.

"Thanks a lot."

"No problem. Good luck."

Caitlin was glad they would be able to get to the crime scene as soon as possible. Speed was key.

This killer had killed twice in a few days—and those were the kills that they knew of. A glance at the wall map reminded her that the rail networks in Ohio were vast, with both used and disused lines crisscrossing the state.

How many more bodies might still be out there, undiscovered, lying on the tracks?

Caitlin grabbed her laptop bag, feeling a sense of urgency as she headed to the door.

CHAPTER FOUR

As Caitlin and Nathan headed to the airport, Caitlin saw that new information was filtering through by the minute. This was a developing case, and she heard her phone pinging with incoming emails and messages as she rushed through the airport with Nathan, heading to the boarding gate for the charter flight they were taking.

The police at both crime scenes were sending the details through to Aniyah, who was immediately forwarding them on. By the time they'd gotten onto the plane and were ready for takeoff, Caitlin was able to piece together a clearer picture.

"Victim number one was Edna Lawson, age thirty-eight. She worked in the nearby town of Lakeview, as an assessor for a local insurance company. She lived with her husband, Brent. He reported her missing yesterday."

"Let's see the pic?" Nathan asked, and Caitlin guessed he was going to look for any physical resemblance with the other victim that the killer might be targeting.

As he searched for it, the plane sped down the runway, and in a few more moments, they were airborne, taking flight through gray, fall skies on the way to the small airport in northern Ohio that was closest to the crime scenes. Caitlin, absorbed in her reading, didn't give more than a quick glance out of the window.

There was the photo of Edna. She was a short, plump woman with a round, cheerful face and a halo of red hair. Caitlin felt a surge of sympathy for her. She looked like a normal, innocent person. Going about her day-to-day life, she had surely not deserved this terrible fate.

"Seems she walked to the bus stop every day to get to and from work, and they believe she must have been grabbed during that walk," Nathan said, reading on.

Caitlin switched to the other, more recent report.

"The second victim was identified as Audrey Carter. Twenty-two years old. She worked part-time at a local catering company. She lived alone but had her driver's license in the pocket of her jeans when she was found."

There didn't seem to be any common factors there. The victims didn't even look similar. Audrey was younger, dark haired, and tall. They worked in different industries and also lived in different small towns that were about eight miles apart.

"There's not much in common at a glance," she said. "I hate to think this is a serial, because his mindset is not evident here."

"We have to see if, and how, these cases are linked." Nathan said.

That was the most important question, Caitlin knew. Why these two? There was a lot of information still to uncover, and the crime scene would provide the first answers. Or so she hoped.

"There are some pointers I can already pick up," Caitlin said, trying to look for the positives, even if they were small. "They're basic but definite. I'm sure you agree on them."

Actually, she wasn't sure at all that they would agree. She was going into untested territory here, that was for sure. Agreeing with Nathan Bridges? That seemed to be something that didn't happen often.

"He's a strong guy." That was the first one she'd had. Surely he couldn't argue that?

"Yes, absolutely. Looking at those crime scenes, they're remote. In the middle of nowhere. The closest parking spot must be a few minutes' walk away. That's a long way when you're carrying a body." Nathan nodded.

They agreed. All good. Caitlin knew that also brought some probable age and size parameters with it. These were fairly broad, but definitely he would be in a good physical condition, fit, and have no damage or injury to his limbs.

But a lot of people fit those parameters. Big guys were not in short supply out in this rural, farming, lumber industry area. On to the next assumption then.

"And he must have his own car."

Now, Nathan was frowning. "Not necessarily."

"Why do you say that? How else could he have grabbed those two women?" Caitlin got herself ready for an argument. This was surely a basic supposition to make. Why was Nathan being so illogical? Were they going to have an argument on the scale of the one they'd had about the office layout a few days ago?

In the end, they had agreed to compromise. But how could you compromise on a theory like this? They needed to get parameters in place that would help them narrow down the MO.

"He could have borrowed a car or hired a car," Nathan said in reasonable tones.

“You think?” She didn’t think it likely.

“He might only have killed them once he got to the railway line itself. They could just have been overpowered until then, tied up on the seat.”

“I don’t think that’s so likely,” she argued.

"If you were a killer not wanting to leave trace evidence, you could do that. In fact, you might seek out ways to do it. And borrowing a car makes it less important to cleanse the trace out, because it’s not your car, right?”

“Surely there’d be some signs,” she protested.

“He could not be using a car at all but be a trucker or a transporter who is using a large vehicle. Maybe he's using a company vehicle, and they don't even know."

Caitlin sighed. All those were in fact logical suppositions. Less likely than having his own car, but not impossible either. How she hated conceding a point.

"Okay," she admitted grudgingly.

"And he's using the train line as a dumping ground. I would say he lives near the tracks, or perhaps he has worked for the railways in the past," Nathan said. “He must have knowledge of them from a personal perspective.”

"No, I disagree," Caitlin countered. She wasn’t going to let Nathan get away with assuming that way. Not when he’d prevented her from doing it.

“Why do you say that?” Now, Nathan was as annoyed as she’d been earlier.

"He could easily have researched where they are located. He could be interested in history or hiking or have lived nearby in the past. Maybe he’s a train spotter."

"Okay," Nathan conceded. "We can agree on that as a possibility."

“At least we’re agreeing,” Caitlin admitted.

Nathan nodded, and she thought he might be suppressing a smile. Serious as this case was, she had to admit, there was some humor in the fact that they were bickering nonstop over details. But at least it meant they were both passionate about their theories.

And at least they were not heading into a standoff, not this time, Caitlin saw. Nathan was conceding points and making good ones. She was ready to concede some herself. Nathan thought very differently from her, but his thinking was logical. She found that having his perspective was helping to broaden her own.

"He's not stupid," she said. "He's not making common mistakes. He's not dropping the body in a place where it will be found quickly. He's dumping them on a remote line where the trains don't stop. He's got it all worked out."

"Yes, I agree with you," Nathan said. "But we still don't know his reasons."

"Nope," Caitlin agreed. And that was the biggest puzzle piece of all to fit in.

Why was he doing this?

If only she knew, Caitlin thought, with a flash of anger at this cowardly killer who was snatching women away and murdering them.

Caitlin continued to read the reports, looking for any further information, any common factors that might allow them to pinpoint this killer. But she couldn't find any. What did the railways signify for the killer, and why had he taken the time to carry, or drag, those bodies there?

Why were these two women dumped on an abandoned rail line? Why not in the woods, or in some out of the way place? This killer must have a reason. This was an important window into his mind, and if she could work out why, then she could find him. Or so she hoped.

CHAPTER FIVE

Nathan Bridges stared out of the window as the airplane prepared to land. He was keen to get to the crime scene and see for himself what it looked like.

What it felt like.

He was a boots-on-the-ground man, always had been in his policing career, and right now, he wanted to put himself in this killer's shoes. He wanted to know what he had experienced when walking along those tracks to choose that spot where he would dump the body.

Ever since he had read the crime scene reports, he had been trying to put himself in that same situation, to imagine what the killer might be thinking.

Nathan knew that getting inside someone’s mind was his weakest point. He was a logistics man who'd used evidence above all else to solve the crimes he'd had success with. He was a people person when it came to successfully dealing with the public. That, he could do, even in a difficult situation. Even if stepping in to defuse a fight put him at personal risk. But thinking like one of these criminals was next level.

But in the last case, he'd watched how Caitlin Dare worked, and he'd seen what it took to tune into the warped and twisted mind of a serial killer. This was new ground for him, and he needed to get to grips with it.

He was fully invested in the success of this case, and he was worried about how much progress they would make and how fast. And there was another practical concern he had, and that was expense.

Being a logistics man, price and costing had always played a key part in his world. As the second in command of his railway policing unit, he'd sat in on the budget meetings and seen his boss's frustration over how they could fit their department's needs into the available budget without compromising their effectiveness.

It had been a tough job. Law enforcement always looked at costs.

Now, here they were, hiring a private airplane so that they could get to the remote crime scene fast. Sure, he knew Aniyah had gotten a few quotes before choosing the most reasonably priced provider, but still, private planes meant money!

And spending money meant justifying the costs.

Nathan knew that they had to do whatever it would take to succeed, to beat this killer, to give families answers, and to save lives, but above all, to prove their worth to those bosses who would be looking at the numbers and going, "should we be spending this?"

The plane touched down on the blacktop of this tiny, local airport with a squeal of wheels. There, in the cloudy, mid-morning gloom, he could see a police car waiting.

He grabbed his bag, put on his jacket, and exited behind Caitlin, thanking the pilot before walking down the steep stairway.

The air felt fresh, clean, with a piney smell from the banks of forest that were swathed to the left of this small airport. The officer waiting for them climbed out of the car. He was a big man in his forties with broad shoulders and a grim expression that Nathan knew had little to do with the cold and everything to do with the two serious crimes in his department's jurisdiction.

"Agent Dare and Officer Bridges," Caitlin said, striding forward to shake hands. It reminded Nathan of the first case when they'd both been feeling insecure and ultra-competitive against each other. At least now they were more of a team, although he really was surprised by how many topics they disagreed on.

It was sometimes worrying to him when he thought about how different they were, but maybe having two polar opposite perspectives was good, Nathan thought.

And at least there was no danger they'd ever bring romantic involvement into the mix, he acknowledged wryly. He was single, having been focusing on his career after a breakup, but he knew Caitlin had a boyfriend who was joining her in her new home city.

Putting that out of his mind, he walked over to greet the cop.

"It's good to have you two here to help out," the cop replied. "I'm Officer Kelvin. You want to go straight to the scene?"

"Yes, please," Caitlin said.

They got into the warmth of the car, where Nathan picked up the distinctive smell of hamburger. The officer had obviously stopped at a local drive-thru on his way to pick them up. Nathan was sure that followed a long, cold, and hungry stint at the crime scene.

"How were the bodies discovered?" he asked.

"The first victim was found yesterday, late evening, by a local woman walking her dog. The dog started pulling in that direction and whining, and the woman took one look at the rags, decided they looked suspicious and smelled bad, and called us without touching the scene," Kelvin explained.

"That was Edna Lawson, the victim that had been reported missing three days ago?" Caitlin clarified.

"Yes. The body was at least two days old, coroner confirmed. Then the other victim, Audrey Carter, was found early this morning. A train driver going the opposite way along the tracks at that junction called it in when he saw it. The track engineer, who's still at the scene I think, went out to look and found it."

Nathan pressed his lips together. Two bodies turning up in two days meant things were extremely serious. He hoped that some answers could be found when they reached the scene. The worry was that more bodies were already out there.

"Have you taken a look at the missing persons reports?" he asked, with that theory in mind.

The officer glanced around at him and nodded. "Yes. We've been through them a few times since last night. We've looked at all towns within a twenty-mile radius."

"And? Anyone else who might turn up on the tracks?"

"There are a couple of unsolved cases, but they are weeks or months old. We're hoping to hell that none of them are involved, and that this guy isn't going to take anyone else."

That was a hope Nathan shared, for sure.

The officer drove out of the airport and stayed on the main road for a couple of miles before peeling off and heading into the deep, quiet countryside.

"How far away from the first site was the other body found?" Caitlin asked.

"About ten miles from here."

That definitely indicated a local killer, Nathan thought. He knew that Caitlin had disagreed on that point, but Nathan felt strongly that this would be someone from the local community and not someone who had just researched where the train tracks were.

As they approached the crime scene, Nathan saw the scattering of cars that indicated a serious crime. Police cars, the coroner's van, and forensic vehicles were all on scene.

Kelvin stopped the car, and they got out. Immediately, Nathan heard the crackle of radios, but it was coming from surprisingly far away. The piney smell was stronger here. He thought he could hear the faraway rattle of a train traversing a distant track.

"This is not an easily accessible area," the police officer explained apologetically. "This is as close as you can get with a car."

To Nathan's surprise, it was a brisk, five-minute walk along a rocky path before the radios grew louder and the scene itself came into view. Finally, they saw the forensic officers, who looked to be standing down. As they arrived, the two men were taking off their gloves and foot covers, speaking quietly to each other as they walked away.

They hurried over to forensics.

"I've got the railway crimes unit here," Kelvin said. "Is there any evidence on the scene, anything left behind by the killer? Footprints, fingerprints?"

The forensic officer shook his head. "The scene's very clean. Coroner is still working, but there's no trace evidence to be found nearby. And we have looked." He glanced tiredly at the other man, and Nathan knew from experience how much brutally hard, detailed work was described in those few words.

"No footprints or fingerprints, and I'm guessing that the killer might have walked for some distance along the actual tracks, which of course would have meant no footprints," the tech confirmed.

Again, Nathan also thought, this meant a physically strong killer.

"And the material the body was wrapped in? Are there any clues from that?"

"Old, half perished tarps and a few felt rags. The kind of thing you'd find in any storeroom. We looked carefully at both scenes, and there's nothing that can tell us where they are from," he said. "No identifying features, no writing, nothing caught in them. And no fingerprints or trace."

"Was the victim clothed?" Caitlin asked.

"Yes, fully clothed, as was the other one, and from the descriptions of the missing people, it seems that they were wearing what they wore when they disappeared."

Nathan nodded. So, the killer was being very careful. And that made their job a whole lot harder. Already, it seemed as if they were going to be stuck with no obvious forensic leads and a shortage of evidence.

But at that moment, the coroner who was working on the body looked up, saw them, and called out, "Railway crime unit? I've just found something here that might help you."

CHAPTER SIX

Helpful evidence?

Caitlin felt eager to know what it was as she rushed over to where the coroner was at work. In the distance, he'd been nothing more than the dark shape of an overcoat with the gleam of a protective head cover above it.

Closer up, she saw he was an older man, with graying hair under that head cover, and sharp, wise eyes behind gold-framed spectacles.

"Good morning," she said, feeling hopeful about this evidence.

"Morning," he said, easing himself up from where he'd been crouched over the body. "I've found something interesting here, on this victim's wrists."

"What is it?" Caitlin asked, stepping forward. As she always did in the presence of the dead, she took a moment to gather her thoughts before looking down at the corpse.

The weight of every death always felt like a physical burden on her shoulders, as well as being a painful reminder that their work was never done, and that evil always lurked. She took in a breath and steadied herself. This was a time for concentrating and finding out what this new evidence was, so that they could save lives.

"See here?" Carefully, the man pushed back the victim's long sleeve. "I've found something that looks like an abrasion mark on each of her wrists. Would you like to take a look?"

Caitlin took her first view of the corpse, looking at the sheet white skin, the wide, staring eyes, and the tangled, dark hair. She felt a huge sympathy for her, having been dumped here by this evil killer. It strengthened her resolve to find out who had done this and to stop them from doing it again. Although at times like this, she couldn't stop herself from feeling helpless and wishing she had powers that offered an instant route to solving the case.

"What is it? Is it a scar from being tied up?" she asked, looking down at the faint but discernible marks.

He nodded. "It looks like some kind of long-term bruising," the coroner told her. "As if the victim had been tied up for some time, probably with nylon rope. I'm guessing she fought it and tried to get out of the ties."

This was interesting, and it might be very important. This victim had not died instantly. Why not? Caitlin wondered. Why had he kept her alive, and where had she been kept?

"Can you tell how long the victim had been tied up?" Caitlin asked.

"A few hours, at least, I would say," he replied.

"Here or elsewhere?"

"There's evidence she was moved after death," he replied, which answered that question.

"And the cause of death?" Caitlin asked. This information hadn't been available when they got on the airplane.

"Cause of death is a powerful blow to the head," the coroner informed her. "It would have been instantly fatal."

"Any other wounds?" Caitlin asked. She was wondering exactly how this had played out and how this victim had gotten the chance to struggle for some time in her nylon rope ties.

"Yes, I am seeing here that there is more than one head injury. She has an abrasion on the side of the head as well."

The information was adding up.

"Is it possible, do you think, that he knocks his victims out, holds them somewhere, and then kills them?"

"Yes, that's very possible. The full autopsy may tell us more, but from my initial exam, that could very well be what he's doing."

But why? Caitlin thought. Why these women, and why this scenario?

Stepping back and letting the coroner do his work, she moved over to speak to the rail engineer who'd found the body. He was standing nearby, talking rapidly on his phone, but he cut the call as she and Nathan approached.

"How can I help you?" he asked somberly.

Caitlin thought quickly. "I'd like to know what time this sighting was called in, and what time you found the body."

"It was called in very early. Someone saw it as they were coming in at about five a.m. and sent out the alert. It was still dark then, so he wouldn't have seen it clearly. I went out at about six, and probably found her at about six-thirty."

He looked sick as he spoke. Caitlin could imagine the shock he'd been in.

"Was there anything suspicious nearby? Did you see or hear anything unusual?"

"No. It was raining heavily, so I was keeping my focus on the track and trying to avoid the worst of the weather," he admitted.

"Had you ever seen the victim before?"

"No, not to my knowledge. When they found out who she was, her name wasn't familiar either."

"Anything else lying around, any markers, any signs?" Nathan asked.

"No. I might have missed something in the rain, but the track was clear apart from this," he said. "There was a loose jointbar, but that's not unusual for this section of track, where the rails are joined."

"Thank you," Caitlin said.

It was time to leave the scene of this crime and go speak to the people who knew the victims.

This was never her favorite part of the job. But they desperately needed to find out what the two women had in common that had led to both of them suffering this tragic, lonely fate.

*

Officer Kelvin got on his radio when they were back at the car and told Caitlin and Nathan that Audrey Carter had lived alone, but that her next of kin, who also lived in the same town, was her older brother, Duke.

"I can take you there to speak to him," he said. "Two police from our department were there an hour ago to break the news, so he knows."

Caitlin nodded, feeling that this was a good first step. Hopefully, if he'd lived in the same town, the brother had regular contact with Audrey and would know what was going on in her life, and if there had been any problems with anyone in town. The timing was not ideal, though.

"We're headed there now," Kelvin said, punching in the address.

Caitlin and Nathan exchanged a look.

"Let's hope he can give us some answers," Nathan said.

"And let's hope it's enough," Caitlin added, before they drove off. She could see that Nathan knew that interviewing someone who had recently heard such shocking news was never going to be optimal. The brother would be in a state of total distress and might not recall every detail clearly.

But as they drove, Caitlin felt her resolve build. This was the first opportunity for a break they would have in the case. If they could learn what had been going on in the lives of these two women, there was a chance they could identify the common factor that she was sure existed.

It took only a few minutes for Kelvin to drive into the small town located on the border of a thick forest.

"Duke works at the local sawmill, but he said he was going to stay home today after hearing the news," Kelvin explained, pulling up outside the simple, single-story house on a corner stand, with woods behind it. "I'll wait in the car, so he doesn't feel too crowded. Let me know if you need me."

Caitlin got out and headed up to the house. She knocked on the door, feeling relieved that Officer Kelvin, correctly in her opinion, felt that the bereaved brother didn't need to be overwhelmed by visitors.

In a few moments, Duke Carter answered the door himself, his eyes red-rimmed, and his face still pale from shock. She could see the family resemblance looking at him, compared to the photos of Audrey she'd seen. He had the same thick, dark hair, high cheekbones, and rangy, tall frame.

He was wearing scuffed, old-looking jeans, and a gray T-shirt she thought he might have slept in.

"I'm Agent Dare, and this is Officer Bridges," Caitlin said. "I'm so sorry for your loss."

Duke nodded, his expression unreadable.

"We want to try and understand why this happened," she said, "and I was hoping you could help us."

"Come in," Duke said, as if remembering this courtesy to visitors almost as an afterthought.

He led the way into a small living room that looked comfortable and messy, with a crocheted rug thrown over the couch, a pair of shoes on the floor, and an empty plate and beer mug on the coffee table. Duke definitely lived alone, Caitlin thought.

"What do you want to know?" he asked, as they all sat down.

"I'd like to know if there was anything going on in Audrey's life," she said.

Duke paused for a moment, then said, "I don't know if I can help you. I spoke to Audrey once or twice a week, and we got together for dinners and drinks, of course, but she didn't tell me about personal issues in her life."

"Work wise, was she happy? Any recent changes?"

"I already told the other detectives about her job," Duke said.

"What about it?" Caitlin asked.

"She hated it," Duke told her. "She was looking to change jobs, and in fact, she'd applied for a few jobs elsewhere, and I think she was even considering a couple of offers."

"Why did she hate it?" Caitlin asked. Had conflict erupted as a result of this hated job?

"Money, mostly," Duke told her. "She said it was too low-paid, and that it was boring. She was a back-office worker, who dealt with the catering company's accounts. But she got on with everyone at work. I mean, why would anyone kill a low-paid employee just because they didn't like their job?"

"Did she have any enemies?" Nathan asked.

Duke shook his head. "No, she was a very friendly person who got along with everyone."

Caitlin looked at Nathan. It seemed clear that Audrey Carter hadn't had any enemies, and if Duke was right, no major stresses or worries either.

"Any boyfriend?" she tried.

"She'd been on a couple of dates recently. She did tell me the names, that I do know. She said it would make her feel safer if I knew when she was heading out on a date with a stranger."

"And who were they?" Caitlin asked.

Clearly unable to remember, he took his phone off the coffee table and scrolled through it with hands that were shaking slightly. "Here they are. This is the message. One was Howard Watts, and one was Alan Arthur. They both live in the county, but the dates were just coffee, and she told me afterward that it didn't seem like either of them were right for her."

"And her friends? Who did she hang out with?"

"She hung out with a few friends from work. She mentioned Patti James quite often, and Annette Edwards, who she knew from church, and she also kept in touch with a guy called Don Andrew, who is a mutual friend. But there were no issues with any of them."

Even so, Caitlin decided that she was going to keep those names in mind. Perhaps one of these potential romantic interests hadn't felt the same way about that "just coffee" date.

To link the killings, though, she'd need to find a thread that connected the other victim, and that was where she needed to go next.

CHAPTER SEVEN

Common threads were now uppermost in her mind, after the evidence Caitlin had obtained so far. Where did they lead, and would the other victim provide a link? Thanking Duke, she and Nathan left the house and hurried back to the car where Officer Kelvin was waiting.

"So, Edna Lawson lived about ten miles away?"

"That's correct. You want to go there now?"

"Let's go there," Caitlin agreed. Climbing in, she consulted her notes again as the car bumped over the uneven side road, heading back to the main road.

No boyfriend, she reviewed, and no work issues. What else was there? There were a few names of friends, a few casual dates. Somewhere in this fragile web of connections, just one strand might stretch over. And if she could find that, she might learn why these two women had died.

She looked out of the window at the passing scenery, the woods and fields and the occasional house, in the pretty countryside that separated these two small towns.

Finally, they reached the house where Edna Lawson had lived with her husband. It was him they would need to speak to now, and Caitlin was not looking forward to the conversation. Bereaved spouses, who had recently heard about the death, were going to be in a world of pain. She would have to step into that world and knew it would awaken all her own fears and memories of Ella.

“The husband’s name is Brent,” Officer Kelvin said. “Brent Lawson.”

“Never my favorite job doing this,” she muttered, and to her surprise, Nathan overheard her.

“Not mine, either,” he said somberly.

The house was an old, two-story colonial, with a porch running almost the length of the front. It was in a neat neighborhood, with manicured gardens and well-kept homes.

Officer Kelvin pulled up, and she and Nathan got out. Sighing, she walked up the path and knocked on the door.

Brent Lawson answered the door a minute later. He looked shocked and pale, and his eyes were red. But he was composed, at least as much as anyone in his position could ever be, Caitlin thought.

This man, with his receding hairline and neatly trimmed, chestnut hair, wearing canvas cargo pants and a company branded top, might just have the answers to this crime.

"We're here to investigate this crime, and I'm so sorry for your loss," she said. "We need to find out what we can about your wife. We are trying to find out if there was anything in her life that could have made her a target."

Brent nodded, but his face was blank. He definitely looked as if he'd disassociated himself from the nightmarish situation in which he'd landed.

"Can we come in?" she asked.

He stepped aside wordlessly, and she and Nathan entered a large, old-fashioned living room. The wood floor was covered with a bright rug, and the furniture looked homey and comfortable.

He sat opposite them. He was twisting his fingers together nervously. Looking at him, Caitlin noted that he didn't just seem distressed about this murder. It seemed like there was more to it. She was sensing it from his demeanor. And sure enough, in a moment, he confirmed it.

"I'm devastated about this," he stammered out. "But you should know, upfront, that we were getting divorced."

"You were?" Nathan sounded incredulous.

"It's true, I can show you the papers," Brent said. "We were married for fourteen years. We were college sweethearts. But we'd been having problems for a couple of years, and I'd been unhappy for the last couple of months."

"Why are you telling us this?" Caitlin asked, trying to keep her tone gentle.

"Because I want you to know that I had no motive," he said. "I had no reason to hurt her. It was an amicable separation. I wanted to try again, but she said it wouldn't work, and I agreed. But I am sure you suspect me. I know the other police did. They asked me the same questions over and over."

"What was going to happen?"

"She was going to move in with one of her girlfriends a few counties away. I mean, she suggested that. She was happy about it, and there was a transfer available through her work that would actually leave her in a better position. We discussed it all. Like I said, it was amicable. We didn't rush into it. We went to counseling; she attended a few support sessions."

"And where were you when she disappeared?"

"I was out of town at a company sales conference in North Dakota. I called her to make sure she was okay because she didn't like spending evenings alone. She didn't pick up, and I got worried, because the neighbors said no lights were on. So, I reported her missing, and since then, I've been feeling worried and guilty that this happened because I wasn't home."

"Did you call her cell?" Nathan asked.

Brent nodded. "Yes, the cell and the landline. Both just rang. I think they're trying to track her cell, but it's off now. I guess it ran out of battery."

"Did you call any of her friends?" Caitlin asked.

"Yes, I called a couple of them, the ones who live near here. None of them knew anything."

"And you have no idea who might have done this?" Caitlin asked.

Brent himself had been out of town, and as the spouse, always a prime suspect, he had an alibi. But now, they needed to know what he knew.

"No, I've been trying to think who it could have been, but I can't think of anyone. I didn't know my wife had any enemies." He looked at them, as though desperate for answers.

"Did she have any problems at work?" Caitlin asked.

"No, she really liked her job, and like I said, when she wanted to move, they found her a new, better job with another branch."

"Any romantic interests? Any new partners or lovers?"

"No, not that I know of at all."

"Did you have any hobbies or interests that you shared with your wife, or that she did on her own?"

"No, we didn't really have anything in common. We went in different directions. I liked to go out and do things, socialize while Edna liked reading and watching TV. I mean, that's okay to live your life that way. It just meant we didn't have much common ground after a while."

"I don't know if you are aware, but there was another similar crime that was discovered this morning," Caitlin said.

"Yes, I heard about that. The first police mentioned it. I was in so much shock at the news, I didn't really understand what they were saying at first."

"Do you know the other victim, Audrey Carter, at all?"

"No, I don't know her."

"I'm going to read out some names to you, and if you do recognize any of them, or if you remember Edna interacting with them, please let me know," Caitlin said.

She began reading the names, slowly, giving the shocked husband time to process each one.

"Howard Watts. Alan Arthur. Annette Edwards. Don Andrew."

Duke listened, shaking his head each time, and when she reached the end of her short list, Caitlin felt disappointed. It was clear there were no common threads, and this meant they were now all stumped for leads.

But then, Brent frowned. It was as if he'd only just realized what Caitlin had said, and as if he'd been in a daze up until that moment. Now, there was a new focus in his eyes.

"Wait a minute. That first name. What was it again?"

"Howard Watts," she said, reading the name of one of the two men that Audrey had been on a date with.

"Howard Watts?" He frowned again, looking perturbed. "I do know him."

"What's the background?" Caitlin asked.

"He's one of Edna's work colleagues. I mean, she's mentioned him in the past, because he was training up to be part of her team."

That rang alarm bells for Caitlin. Loud ones too. This was a recent connection, who had just moved into the lives of both the victims.

He'd dated Audrey once. He was training up in Edna's work team. This was the only connection between the victims they'd been able to identify. Had both of them been targeted by a psychopath they'd crossed paths with?

It was time to find out.

CHAPTER EIGHT

He liked to think of himself as their last chance saloon. Yup, that was who he was. The last time they had to rethink their lives. And it was up to them. All up to them.

It was a big part of his message—the critical moment when they realized their error. When they knew they'd made a mistake. A big mistake. And it would be all up to them, whether they went down the wrong path or took the right one.

He gave them the choice, and it was a fair choice. He was an honest man. All that he could do was save them from the terrible regret and sadness of picking the wrong path. But that was meaningful to him. Saving people from their own bad choices was a selfless act, he thought.

He was a man on a mission, the kind of mission that might gradually change the world, and maybe even save it.

Now, he pulled into the parking lot of the big shopping mall and got out of his car. People were pouring into the mall, and he realized that he'd picked a good day to do this. A Thursday. It was a popular day for shopping, and there was a lot of foot traffic in the mall.

"This is an excellent start, and we're set up for success," he said to no one in particular.

The words were only important to him, to prepare him as he got ready for this exciting mission ahead.

"Yes, it's going to work out well," he reinforced to himself. "There should be no problem with helping this next person."

He smiled as he thought about the satisfaction that the help would bring. To him, of course. If they chose wrong, they would be dead. But death was far better than the bad consequences. It was a kinder choice, all the way.

He still remembered the light he'd felt in his mind when the first chance had come along. It felt as if a puzzle piece that he didn't even know he'd been seeking had slotted into place. He'd realized, with a warm glow, how pivotal he could be in their lives.

Of course, his mission was far from easy. When he looked at the choices and the consequences, he'd been angry at first, so very angry at what they were planning. He'd felt appalled by their recklessness, saddened and worried. But now, he was calmer. Now, he knew what he was doing, and he could take comfort from the end result he was able to give them. It was always good to hear their answers. And he knew the questions, the ones that were important. He enjoyed asking them, even if it was difficult at the time. He was a patient man.

"Excuse me," an elderly woman asked him as she tottered into the mall.

"How can I help?" he asked, with a friendly smile.

"I'm looking for the bookstore."

"I'm going in that direction myself," he said. He even took her arm as he walked carefully along beside her.

People might think him to be a monster, this he knew. But look at him now, helping an old lady on her way. Of course, he had no problems with the elderly. They'd lived their lives and were entitled to whatever choices and conclusions they wanted. It was the younger ones, the people in their twenties, thirties, forties, and even fifties, that he felt himself compelled to save.

There were so many people who needed saving. He was beginning to realize that although he'd started small, this could end up big. Really big.

It was a joy to realize the power he had. Mr. Last Chance. And he liked to think that he exercised that power fairly. He was not an unfair man.

"Careful," he said, guiding his elderly companion down the ramp that he thought would be easier for her than the few stairs that were the other choice. You see, so easily, a better choice had been made.

Again, he thought of all the other people who'd been on that first step, but who had sadly taken the wrong path. He thought of their poor, sad faces and their miserable, lonely lives. And he remembered the good feeling he got when he could help them. Best of all, he didn't feel a shred of guilt about it. Why would he when he was saving them from an unspeakable alternative?

Here was the bookstore.

"Are you okay from here?" he asked.

"I am. Thank you so much. You're very kind," she smiled, and he glowed at the praise. Now, where was the man he needed? Mr. Last

Chance had known he was going to be in this part of the mall now, and he had thought this would be an excellent opportunity to grab him.

He was looking forward to finding out more about him. The questions seethed in his mind. In fact, his new passion was making him feel fanciful. In earlier days, he would have been an interrogator, one of those respected and feared, used by kings and lords and leaders. But now, in today's modern world, he liked to think he came across as approachable.

Of course, the settings he had to choose for the job were not ideal, not what he would have preferred, but that was beyond his control. When the wrong answer, their wrong choices, meant putting an instant end to their folly, you could not exactly ask the questions sitting across from the person in a coffee shop.

He laughed at the thought. But then, quickly contained the laughter. It was wrong to laugh. People were so wedded to their choices, but it was not actually funny. Rather, it was sad. Ideally, it would never reach the stage where he had to take such drastic action.

And there was his target. Leaving the coffee shop where he'd been having a meeting. That was him. Dark hair, a brown jacket, and pale gray chinos. A very ordinary looking man, but someone who was about to have an extraordinary moment of clarity about his life.

He'd expected the man to leave the mall and was surprised when he veered into a stationery store. Sidling along behind, he watched him carefully. What was he doing there?

He was buying a briefcase. Hmmm. Was that a clue? That could go either way. It wasn't enough of a pointer to his decision. It still gave Mr. Last Chance no real leads. It was all going to be so exciting when he finally got to the truth!

He could see the man struggling to decide which one to buy. It seemed like he had difficulty with decisions in general, the man thought, with some sympathy for that trait. It was not always easy to choose right.

"It's not, is it? So often, you can go down the wrong track," he said aloud. And then, because nobody else was doing it, he answered himself. "The wrong track, yes. And it's not so easy to reverse back along that track once you've done it!"

He watched closer now, feeling rather invested in this entire process, as if he was shopping by proxy. The man took his time, occasionally glancing at the other customers in the shop, but with a look that said he was thinking more than he was watching.

Finally, he decided and approached the checkout. He handed over the cash.

Mr. Last Chance followed him as he left the store, and he noted that the man was not walking quickly. He was not in a hurry. It looked like he was going home, but not in haste. He definitely had no urgent destination in mind.

He looked distracted, thoughtful, as if he was pondering his life and his choices. More than once, in fact many times, he glanced at his cellphone, and Mr. Last Chance wondered if this was because he was expecting something to arrive. A message, a call, a confirmation. Perhaps this would give him a pointer. He watched intently.

Sure enough, the man grabbed his phone and read the incoming message intently. He nodded. His movements and his body language now looked more decisive. For sure, he was now set on a path.

"That's good," he murmured. "That's good for you."

A good decision? Or a bad one?

It seemed like he had a lot on his mind. He hoped that the man's own judgment would guide him correctly. Or perhaps he'd gotten some good advice through that text.

But then again, he thought, it was often the case that people were too stubborn to take the right path before it was too late.

He still had no idea which path it would be. At any rate, it confirmed to him what he had suspected. And that was this—his intervention was going to take place at exactly the right time.

The man left the mall and walked to his car, briefcase in hand, a thoughtful expression on his face.

Mr. Last Chance followed behind, ready to grasp an opportunity that he was sure would be there in the next minute. The car was all the way at the back of the lot, and he didn't see anyone else around.

He'd parked just a few bays away. Mr. Last Chance smiled again, and this time, there was a lot less warmth in the expression as he increased his speed.

CHAPTER NINE

Now highly suspicious of Howard Watts's connection to both victims, Caitlin wondered if living and working so close to both of them had been why he'd targeted these two women. After all, he lived in the same suburb as Audrey Carter, which also happened to be the place where Edna Lawson's work offices were based.

This meant that to speak to him, they needed to retrace their steps to the company premises in South Clearwell.

"You're welcome to use the car from here on. We can sign it out to you at the local police department," Officer Kelvin invited them.

They pulled over at the police station and climbed out to finalize the paperwork. As Caitlin walked with the two men to the entrance, her phone rang.

She grabbed it, her blood pressure spiking as she worried this might be a further development on the case, such as another body being found. That was her biggest fear. A ringing phone at this point brought a thousand worries.

But the number was not Aniyah from the office. It was an unfamiliar cellphone number, and when she answered, she found herself speaking to a man she'd never heard before.

"Is that Ms. Caitlin Dare?" the man said, his voice sharp and businesslike.

What was this about? she wondered.

She hung back, allowing the two men to walk into the police station while she stayed outside, standing on the paved path, flanked by the neatly trimmed grass that fronted the building.

"Yes, that's me. Who's speaking please?" she challenged.

"It's Attorney Phil Jonson here. I'm calling on behalf of Joshua Dare."

Uncle Josh? Nerves clenched Caitlin's stomach. Uncle Josh was getting a lawyer involved? He'd hinted at doing exactly that during their confrontation last week.

"And why are you calling, Mr. Jonson?" she demanded, swallowing down the sense of dread that her uncle's name had automatically brought.

"You arrived on Mr. Dare's doorstep last week. You made a series of threats and allusions about him."

"I did not!" Caitlin protested. "I was there to ask questions."

"That's not what my client has indicated to me," Jonson said, his voice calm. "My client has indicated that you have been harassing him, falsely accusing him of a serious crime, and invading his privacy."

"What?" Caitlin gasped, feeling outraged.

"He has asked me to warn you off," Jonson continued. "Please desist immediately with these false accusations. If you continue, my client will take legal action. I am calling you to say that we are going to send you a cease-and-desist letter, both via email and also physically, in person."

"I'm not home! I'm out of town on a case!" Caitlin snapped, but her stomach was twisting hard now.

"Then we will deliver it when you are home. Should you continue this harassment, we will be applying for a restraining order against you. Kindly confirm if this is your correct email address?"

He read it out.

This was progressing fast. She was speeding toward an unwanted outcome. This was not the time to cause more trouble, she sensed. And right now, there was nothing she could do. There was no point in coming across as hardcore. It wasn't intimidating this man in the slightest.

In a resigned voice, she gave the lawyer her updated email address and her physical address.

"I would like you to understand that I arrived at his house to ask questions, and I did not expect to be intimidated by legal action. I'm entitled to ask questions," she countered when she'd given the information.

"I can't comment on that, ma'am," Jonson said. "I can only reiterate what my client has told me. He feels that you're not acting rationally, and in fact, you seem to have become delusional. He is ready to take legal action, and if you continue to harass him, he will issue a restraining order against you. I have no ax to grind with you, I have no personal agenda, but I can tell you that my client is one hundred percent committed to his course of action. You'd do well to keep that in mind, ma'am."

And with that, to Caitlin's consternation, he hung up.

She was left gasping in anger and outrage. Uncle Josh had completely turned the tables on her. Never mind evading her questions, now he was actually on the attack.

She had no idea what it meant. Did it mean he was completely guilty and just looking to deflect her from probing any deeper? Or did it mean he was genuinely innocent, and he just couldn't take the accusations anymore? He'd made it look as if she was the one doing the harassing, and he was the victim, who needed protecting.

Had he really seemed like an innocent man when she'd confronted him last week? She'd been so angry, so full of wrath and ready to accuse him, that she had not been able to tell.

She shook her head, as if she could shake away these unpleasant thoughts. They were not helpful to her now, not when she needed to focus on the case. That needed to be her priority. And the debacle that was unfolding with her uncle would have to be shelved until the case was done.

Nathan was walking out now, with the car keys in his hand, and it was time to go and talk to Howard Watts.

Putting a lid on her emotions once and for all regarding Uncle Josh, Caitlin hurried to join him.

She was glad that they were now on their way. It meant that she could focus on the matter at hand, and she would not be distracted by her uncle's phone call.

They had a lot to discuss. For example, what did they know about Howard Watts?

"He seems to have been working for Brooks Insurance Brokers for just five months," Nathan said, reading his phone. "Aniyah sent more information on him now."

Caitlin guessed that would also have come through to her phone, and if she hadn't been so sidetracked, she would have read it too.

"Five months is a short timeframe. What was he doing before that?" she asked.

Nathan handed her the keys, and she got in the driver's seat, heading for South Clearwell.

"Before that, he doesn't seem to have lived locally," Nathan said. "It looks like he only moved here a few months ago, from a town in the south of the state. I don't see any reasons for the move, but I guess we can ask him."

There was a lot to ask, Caitlin knew, as she set off, speeding along the road before peeling off in the direction of the town's small financial center. Here, in a three-story office block, the insurance company was located.

She parked outside, and they walked in. Caitlin went straight up to the reception desk.

"Agent Dare and Officer Bridges. I'm looking for Howard Watts. Is he here? It's police business. We need information from him on a case," she explained.

The receptionist frowned. "Is this to do with Edna's murder? Because we're all totally devastated by it."

"Yes, it is," Caitlin said, feeling sympathetic about the waves the crime had made.

"I'm not sure if he's in. I'll have a look on the computer and see if he's scheduled for anything."

While she tapped the keyboard in front of her, Caitlin glanced around. The area was tidy, with blue carpets and navy and white striped furniture and paintings on the walls that were pretty, forgettable prints of boats and seascapes and trees. Everything was neat and businesslike, but at the same time, it was a small set of offices for a corporate environment. She wondered if that made it more likely that Edna had been targeted by a colleague.

The receptionist turned back to them. "Howard Watts is upstairs. I can ask him to meet you in a meeting room now?"

"That sounds great," Caitlin confirmed, pleased that they were going to be getting ahead with this.

The receptionist pressed more buttons and spoke briefly, "Meeting room one, on the second floor," she told them.

They headed upstairs and walked into the meeting room, which was the closest room to the elevators and stairwell and looked to be followed by an enormous, open plan office. The meeting room was decked out in muted shades of beige, with an eight-seater table, a big screen, and comfortable office chairs.

Caitlin didn't close the door. She wanted to check who was walking past, thinking of all those offices, and that Howard Watts might not actually want to speak to the police. Quickly, she glanced down at her own phone, looking at the information Aniyah had sent through and confirming what Howard looked like. Appearance could already give them a clue.

He was tall, six-foot-one, with curly, brown hair and a big, solid build, she saw from the photos. Physically, he could be their guy.

She didn't necessarily trust that a man who was guilty of murder might arrive at the meeting room, ready and willing to talk to the police. She thought a man like that would be more likely to make a run for it.

And at that exact moment, she heard footsteps thundering along the corridor, heading away from the open plan offices and toward the exit points. A tall man flashed past the open door, making for the steps at a run.

Feeling anxious now, Caitlin jumped up and rushed outside.

CHAPTER TEN

She'd thought it was Howard Watts, and this sight confirmed it. Caitlin saw to her consternation, a tall, six-foot man with curly, brown hair and a heavy, strong build was running down the corridor in the opposite direction to the meeting room.

"Hey!" she yelled, without even taking the time to tell Nathan what she was doing. All there was time for now was to act. This guy was the suspect, she was sure of it, and he was making impressive speed in his rush for the exit.

He looked around, skidding to a stop, and she saw his face change, anxiety replacing the intent expression she'd noticed there.

"Uh—hi," he said, turning. His face was flushing red.

"Are you Howard Watts? What are you doing? Where are you going? We're waiting in here for you!" As she spoke, Caitlin strode toward him. No way was he making a run for it now. She'd chase him down and blockade the parking lot exit.

Behind her, Nathan was at the meeting room door, peering out into the corridor, looking as intent as Caitlin felt.

"I—er—yes. I'm Howard."

"Why were you going to the exit?"

He'd been caught out, and now he was embarrassed. He fidgeted uneasily, his chunky fingers twining together. "I must have gotten it wrong. I thought I was supposed to meet you downstairs."

"In here, please," Caitlin said firmly. She felt damned lucky to have been checking those exits. No way was this just an innocent mistake. She was convinced that he had been trying to quickly disappear from the building, rather than be questioned by police.

Then, the next moment, a surprising shiver of doubt chilled Caitlin as she remembered her recent call from the lawyer. Perhaps she had lost her ability to make judgment calls in these situations and was genuinely making something out of nothing here. Perhaps he really had been going downstairs.

A brief flare of frustration filled her. It wasn't characteristic for her to doubt herself. Her confidence in her work was one of her biggest points of pride, and now Uncle Josh was causing her to falter in that regard. And she hated it.

Well, she'd just have to fight against it, Caitlin reminded herself, and not let her obnoxious uncle get inside her head that way.

"I'm sorry. Not sure what happened. I am fairly new here, you see." Howard explained himself in a steady voice, staring in wide-eyed innocence at Caitlin, but she didn't trust him at all. Fairly new? He'd worked here for months. He must have passed that meeting room every single day.

"Come in, please," she said. He walked in and sat down opposite them.

He wore a plaid shirt with the collar unbuttoned, dark chinos, and she saw a phone stuck into his back pocket. At first glance, he was all the keen, young exec. But there was a look in his eyes that told her this man disrespected law enforcement. He wasn't taking this meeting seriously. She could see that clearly, and since his colleague—in fact, his boss—had been murdered, that was suspicious.

Not to mention that he'd been on a date with Audrey also.

"I'm obviously very upset about Edna," he said, as if reading Caitlin's mind. Too little, too late, she thought.

"Are you?" Nathan asked, leaning forward.

"Yes. We'd been friends, and we were working well together. I hadn't heard from her all day yesterday or the day before. None of us knew where she was, and I was expecting her to come in. I was shocked to hear she had been murdered."

He didn't sound very torn up about it, though.

"You've been working here for months. Did you have any disagreements with Edna?"

"No, we worked well together. Anyone will tell you," he said.

"Why did you move to this area?"

"My father moved. He got transferred. I'm twenty-four and live at home for now, so I decided this was a good opportunity to start out with a proper career."

"You know Edna was leaving town?"

"She had spoken about it. I wasn't aware she'd decided for sure, but I mean, we were all prepared for her to make that move."

"What about Audrey Carter?" she asked, watching him carefully. His big, fleshy hands, which were clasped together, tightened slightly.

"What about her?" he asked. For the first time, he looked genuinely nervous.

"She's dead. She was a victim too. You know that, right?"

Caitlin saw a flicker of emotion cross his face.

"Audrey? No, I didn't know that at all. I had no idea she was killed. I mean, it's horrific, but I barely knew her. We went on one date, that's all, if it's the same Audrey I'm thinking of."

His words were flat and calm sounding, but behind them, she wondered what he was concealing. He was hiding his true emotions, and she wasn't sure why.

"Did you have an argument with her?" she asked. "Did you get in touch at all after the date?"

"No, I didn't."

"You realize how it looks, that you were in contact with both these victims before they died?"

"I don't care how it looks!" He slammed his hands suddenly down on the table, and the crashing noise filled the room. "And I really resent that you're implying I'm a killer. This is a small town! There's probably like a hundred people just in this town who must have known both of them."

"Yes, but you're the one who's been verifiably in contact with both of them recently." Nathan pressured him. They were both out to take this to the max.

"I'm not a killer!" Howard said. "I had no reason to kill Edna. We were working brilliantly together, and I had no reason to hate her!" He half rose from his chair.

"Why are you so upset now?" Caitlin asked. "Why weren't you upset earlier when I told you Audrey had died? You only got upset when I started talking about your reputation, and how it looks that you were connected with both victims."

"I—look, I don't show emotion very well," Howard said. "I never have done. It's my personality. I bottle things up and then I get angry. That's what is happening now."

"So, why did you run away from the meeting room when we arrived?" Caitlin asked.

"I … I got it wrong."

"You were running for the stairs. You didn't get it wrong. That was an excuse. You were avoiding us." Nathan leaned even further forward, his strong arms crossed on the table, his face right in Howard's space.

"Okay. Full disclosure. I didn't want to be involved in this. I'm worried about how it will look for me at work. People will talk." Now, Howard sounded breathless.

"So, your work reputation is more important than finding her killer?" Nathan asked. Before Howard could respond, he shook his head. "Never mind. Rather tell us about your movements last night. From about four p.m. onward."

Audrey had caught the bus home and she'd then disappeared. So, Howard needed to account for all of his time, from then on. There mustn't be a window where he might have done this deed.

"Yesterday, I was in a late meeting," Howard said. "We had to meet up after work because of Edna being away. She'd planned a big presentation, and it was up to us to try and take it forward because we didn't know where she was."

"What time did the meeting start?"

"Straight after work, at half past four."

"And what time did it end?" Caitlin pressured him.

"It ended at about ten. I can show you the code I got when I clocked out of the building. And we ordered snacks and drinks at nine. I took care of that and have all the phone calls to show for it."

"And what did you do after that?" she asked.

"I went home, and I took my dog for a walk in the park. My parents were out. My dad is also working late, and they had a dinner to go to. I went for a walk, because I felt I needed some time to think about the new project and how we were going to do it without Edna here."

Caitlin handed him a sheet of paper.

"Write down all the names of who was at the meeting," she said. "You, your other colleagues, and who else was in the meeting. And write down the time, and who left first and who left last."

He wrote it down, and when he'd finished, he handed it over.

Caitlin thought that this page actually did clear him. He'd been in the meeting with several others. It had been a big meeting. Obviously, they would check and confirm, but if everything added up, then without a doubt, his time was accounted for.

"Fine," she said. "We'll check your alibi, so please do not leave town until you hear from the local police that you are cleared. But if you do have any information that you think might be helpful, then you need to tell us. Any small detail could lead us to the killer. I know you're unhappy that we're questioning you, but that's just the way it is."

"I don't know anyone who would want to hurt her." He spread his hands innocently.

Caitlin sighed. This suspect had an alibi, and he had no further information to offer them. It was now midafternoon, and they were back where they started.

"Okay. You can go now," she said.

Then, her phone beeped, and she glanced down, her focus sharpening as she saw it was Mike messaging her. Had he found a job? Had he spoken to the principal at that high school? She opened it feeling positive and expectant.

The only problem was that the text didn't make sense. Not at all.

CHAPTER ELEVEN

Caitlin frowned down at the text Mike had sent.

"CU later, looking 4wd! xxx"

It was totally confusing. Why had he sent it? Was he going to stay around after all? Did he have positive news he wanted to tell her in person? The problem was that she had no guarantee this case would be wrapped up today. Already, it was late afternoon. Quickly, she texted back to him.

"Great, until when are u in town? Will be back 2morrow."

And then, seeing he wasn't replying immediately, she refocused, turning her thoughts and energy away from Mike and away from the disappointment of interviewing Howard Watts. His alibi ruled him out as a suspect, and they needed to keep looking. She had an idea of the direction she thought they should take next.

"I'd like to go and speak to the first witness," she said to Nathan.

"The dog walker? Why?" Nathan asked. Caitlin bristled. Already, she could see Nathan disagreed with this idea. "Won't the police have interviewed her? She did give a statement I recall," he said.

"Yes," Caitlin said. "She did give a statement."

"So, why are we rushing off to speak to her?" he asked.

Biting back an angry response, she answered in a sweetly sarcastic tone, "Do you have any better ideas to fill up an afternoon that suddenly seems quite free?"

For some reason, she found herself wanting to poke holes in Nathan's easy confidence. What with Uncle Josh's threats and lawyering up and the weird text she'd just gotten from Mike, with no reply from him to her question, she felt unsettled. She was having a bad day. He was just having a normal day! And she wasn't going to let him shoot down her theories without having some of his own to replace them.

Nathan scowled, picking up the insulting tone of her words, but Caitlin didn't care. If he was going to start arguing, he needed to have better ideas.

"I'm sure I can think of something," he said. "But seriously, why her?"

"Because she's a local, and she obviously walks in the area. She might have seen or heard something—if not this time, then maybe another time. She might have remembered it now. Finding a body is a shock, and people don't always think straight at the time. We can't rule out that he spent time in the area before he dumped his victims. He might have needed to check out the dumping site, especially seeing it's probably a fair walk from a road."

"Good point," he said. He stood up from the boardroom desk where they were still seated, brushing his hands on his pants, his broad shoulders flexing as he stretched. "Let's go then."

No fight?

It seemed there was to be no fight. Nathan had agreed.

Caitlin felt strangely deflated. She'd been fully revved up to justify herself and attack his argument if he felt differently. Now, it seemed, they were just going to go straight to this witness's house.

"I feel it's important," she said, just to emphasize the point.

"Absolutely," he replied, and Caitlin cast him a suspicious glance. What was he doing, changing his mind, and agreeing with her so suddenly? It was like he was saving something up for later.

She walked out of the insurance company's offices, noticing that a lot of other people were doing the same. It was heading toward four p.m. Luckily this was a small town, Caitlin thought, because at least afternoon traffic wouldn't be too bad.

And it was for the same reason that she was eager to interview this suspect. It wasn't like this was a huge city. In a smaller town, people knew what was going on.

For all she knew, this dog walker might have even innocently seen and recognized the killer.

*

Half an hour later, they reached the small, neat, suburban home where Mandy Slater lived. It was a typical starter home for a young couple, Caitlin thought. Probably built in the sixties, it looked to have been renovated recently with a fresh and clean feel. There were two small cars parked outside the home, and Caitlin also noticed a dog kennel in the fenced yard.

She knocked on the door, glancing at Nathan out of the corner of her eyes. He was looking as focused and determined as she felt.

From inside, she heard the sound of a dog barking. An excited, enthusiastic bark.

The door swung open, and Caitlin saw that Mandy was a strawberry blonde, petite and pretty, and the dog was a friendly looking animal that looked like a German Shepherd mix.

Pretty as she might be, but Mandy looked stressed, as if finding a corpse on her calm evening dog walk had pushed her right out of her comfort zone. Behind her, Caitlin saw a tall, slim man a couple of years older, hovering anxiously around. He was holding a spatula and judging from the cooking smells emanating from the kitchen, he was playing a role in getting dinner under way.

She got the immediate impression that he was a caring man. Her mind flashed back to her own relationship with Mike for one wayward moment, and Caitlin wondered if their dynamic would ever achieve this level of peaceful harmony.

Then the next moment she scolded herself fiercely for even having thought that while she was on a case. Plus, first impressions didn't always tell the true story, she remembered, gathering her thoughts.

"Sorry to disturb you," she said as a formality. "We're from the railway task force, and we have some questions for you as the witness who found Edna's body."

"Oh," Mandy said. She glanced at her boyfriend, who gave her a reassuring nod. "Sure."

"Come in," he added, and they walked into a small home that smelled deliciously of browning beef, garlic, and—Caitlin thought hungrily—baking bread. The dog sniffed her hand in a friendly way, and she stroked his head.

They all sat down in the small living room, with an open book on the coffee table, the television on, and two glasses of half-finished wine on the sideboard. Quickly, Mandy muted the TV.

"What happened that evening?" Caitlin asked.

"Oh, I don't remember much," Mandy said, looking distressed.

Nathan leaned forward. "Take your time and just tell us what you remember."

"I was walking Harry, our dog, at around five p.m. in the evening. I took a longer route because I'm trying to get fitter. I saw the bundle on the track, and it wasn't really how it looked, it was more how Harry reacted."

"He went crazy, didn't he, babe?" the boyfriend asked, before getting up and rushing through to the kitchen.

"Yes, he started barking and whining and pulling me in that direction. I saw that … that wrapped up bundle, and I just didn't like anything about it. It seemed like it was out of place, and I even thought that it smelled bad too. So, I pulled Harry away, and I immediately called the police. And then I called Gav, to come and walk me home. I was feeling very freaked out. I haven't been that way since then. I've totally changed my route, and I'm not going for long enough to get home in the dark either."

"It's definitely made both of us more cautious," Gav agreed, rushing back from the kitchen again.

"Did you see anything unusual? Hear anything?"

"Not really. I wasn't focusing on my surroundings, though, but more on Harry, because he's a young dog and he's exuberant. He pulls. And I'm trying to voice train him."

"Did you notice any vehicles near the railway track? Any people walking along the tracks, or nearby?"

"No. No, I didn't," Mandy said.

"How about a vehicle when you were walking home? Did you see anything?"

"Well, I waited for the police and for Gav to arrive and by then it was fully dark, so we went home using his flashlight. It was scary. And we didn't notice anything. I was just glad I had my phone with me."

"Yes, it's a good thing you started carrying it," Gav agreed.

"Why did you do that?" Caitlin asked.

"Because—well, I haven't seen them, but we learned from our local community message board that there are some drifters and homeless people who've moved up into that area, into the abandoned cars on the old part of the tracks. And there was that incident a while ago that everyone got nervous about. So, I decided I needed to be more careful. That's why I don't go walking after dark anymore, and why I always take Harry with me." She petted the dog.

Caitlin felt very glad that she'd asked that question, and that she'd come here.

Drifters and homeless people could easily have committed these crimes, or else, seen the person who did.

“What incident is this that people got nervous about?” she asked.

“It was one of the drifters. He lit a fire close to the track and a rail engineer told him to move, to get away. And he didn’t move. Instead, he attacked the engineer and tried to hit him with a metal pipe.”

“Can I see those messages?” Caitlin asked.

They needed to read them and get up to those abandoned cars. As soon as possible, and preferably before dark.

CHAPTER TWELVE

Pierre Allnutt opened his eyes. Not that it helped, because it was completely dark outside.

He felt utterly confused. The first thing that registered in his mind was that he had a splitting headache. This was more than just a headache. Murky memories surfaced, fragmented, and confused. He'd been walking back to his car after being in the mall, and he'd heard footsteps behind him.

He'd looked around, and for one horrified moment, he'd been sure that he was going to be attacked, because he'd seen someone plunging toward him, brandishing … something.

Pierre wasn't sure what. All he knew was that it now felt as if a spike had been lodged in his skull, and putting two and two together, he must have been attacked.

But where was he now?

He couldn't even stretch out a hand to find out. When he tried to push himself off the cold, dark floor, he realized his wrists were tied together behind his back with a smooth, taut rope.

Now feeling seriously scared, Pierre struggled against that rope. Struggled hard.

But it held.

"Help, someone, please!" he shouted. "Help!"

The darkness around him was total, and it felt like a tomb. His heart beat faster, and he struggled harder.

There was no way he could get out of this. He was tied up, and the place was too dark for him to see anything. He was pushed up against a cold metal wall that felt pocked with rust.

Was he in a container, a railway car, even an abandoned steel shed? There was no sound from outside, apart from the usual sounds of the forest. No cars, he realized.

The ropes were tight and digging into his skin with just enough roughness to rub and make things worse. Pierre was starting to panic.

He was a six-foot-tall guy, twenty-five years old, and in good shape. Whoever had brought him here must be strong.

And, with a sick feeling, he realized they were coming back.

He heard footsteps and then a light shone into his eyes, making him cry out and flinch away.

It was bright, painful, and dazzling, and he had no idea who was behind it.

Then a voice, low and raspy, sounded in the gloom. "Pierre?"

"Yes, that's me." His own voice was very hoarse and surprisingly weak. He felt dizzy and nauseous, and he couldn't think straight. His mouth was dry, and he wanted to throw up. This was like a nightmare.

"What is this?" he stammered. "Help me! Get me out of here!"

There was a pause, and with a chill, Pierre realized that this person must be, could only be, the one who'd put him in here.

"Do you know who I am?" the voice asked. Pierre guessed it belonged to a man in his thirties or forties. He wasn't good with ages. It didn't take much skill to surmise the owner of the voice was big and strong.

"How should I know? I don't know a thing! I've been kidnapped. I need help! Help!" he shouted, fear flaring.

There was silence in response, and that glare of the flashlight.

"Calm down!" the voice said sternly. "I'm telling you to calm down or else things will go very badly for you. I'm the person who's in charge of your future. Calm. Down. Now."

The words were spoken with aggressive authority and intent. Gasping, still panicking inwardly, Pierre tried to get a hold on his emotion and fear.

"Why are you doing this?" Pierre asked in a shaking voice.

"Because I need to know the truth, and I need you to tell me."

"The truth about what?" His voice rose hysterically. "I'm being abducted for what truth? What is this?"

He heard the voice sigh. It had a slight accent that he couldn't place, and it was raspy, as if he had a sore throat.

"The truth about what you're planning."

Pierre's hands were behind his back. He could feel his pulse thudding in them, and his heart beating in his throat. It was a stupid question, and he knew it, but he couldn't think straight, and he was scared.

"I'm not planning anything," Pierre said, now feeling angry, partly because it was a reaction to his fear. "Let me out of here, or you'll be sorry."

The man laughed—a cold, hard laugh that was like a crack of ice snapping against old stone.

"You don't get it at all," said the man. "You're alone in this. No one is going to come and rescue you. You're in trouble, Pierre Allnutt. Big trouble. Unless you answer me. What are you planning?"

"Uh," Pierre said. He really didn't know what to do or how to respond to this. Because now that his thoughts were coming back to him, there was something he was planning, although few people knew about it.

"Well, there's obviously that … that, er," he said.

"There's no time for guessing," the man snapped. "And you may as well tell me the truth, because I'll find out anyway, and when I do, it's going to go very badly for you."

"Okay," Pierre capitulated. "There's a new foreman in the factory where I work, and he asked me to be part of a scam. I mean, it's not even really a scam. It's innocent. Just getting rid of the broken items of machinery, helping them find a new home, unofficially. That's all it is."

"Good," the man said.

Pierre suddenly realized that there was something very strange about this conversation. "Did you just say good? You mean, you're not angry?"

The man snorted. "Of course, I'm angry. But if you tell me the truth, that makes it easier. I'm not interested in that scam. It's not what I want to know. Now tell me what your real plans are."

This conversation was so weird, it felt surreal. Perhaps he was dreaming, Pierre suddenly thought. He swallowed and felt his throat click. He had a horrid sense of unreality, as if he was talking to a ghost. He didn't know how much this man knew, and he couldn't lie. His head was too darn sore to come up with a lie.

"You mean, moving in with my girlfriend?" he asked incredulously. "Is that what you mean?"

"That's it. Pierre, you're starting to make sense. And you're lucky. I'm grateful you told me this and didn't just keep lying."

"Uh, I guess." Pierre couldn't quite believe what he was hearing. This man was out of his mind, delusional. He had no idea how he'd heard about this, but now he was quizzing him as if it actually mattered to him.

"I know," the man said. "I don't blame you. It's not your fault you were placed in this position." Pierre heard what sounded like a sigh and a rustle of cloth. The man must have been sitting down.

"Am I right? Are you going to make the move and move in with her?"

"Yeah, sure. I think it's going to go okay. I mean, we've been dating a few months. She's still kind of hung up on her ex which is part of the reason I want to move in. Just in case, you know. Not that I'm a jealous guy of course." He was babbling now in his fear, letting everything out.

"So, you're going to go to a different town?"

"I guess so. Look, to be honest, it's not that far away. I won't have to stop doing my work, or anything. We'll just be living together, and I'll be in a position to take more care of her, and of course, to see if her ex shows up."

The man sighed. He sounded disappointed. "How I wish you'd made a different choice. You could have gone either way with this. You chose the wrong way."

His voice was harsh.

"What are you doing?" Pierre felt suddenly terrified at the change in his tone, the helplessness of his predicament.

The beam shone again, pinning him in its ice white glare.

"I'm putting you out of your misery," the man said.

There was a clang and a crash and then Pierre screamed.

It was a scream of shock and of horror. But it was cut short, and suddenly, the world went dark.

CHAPTER THIRTEEN

Half an hour later, the sun was setting, managing to break through the gloomy clouds with faint rays of red and gold. As she and Nathan walked up to the dilapidated railway cars on the hill, Caitlin felt grateful for any light that cut through the shadows.

This was too important to set aside for tomorrow, but already, it was getting dark. Darkness was not their friend here in this deserted area, where an aggressive wanderer, an off-the-grid person or perhaps a vagrant, had set up his home.

She pulled her flashlight out of her jacket pocket, and Nathan clicked on his.

The cars loomed ahead of them, dark and shadowy in the bobbing beams. The beam illuminated their dark sides, the rusting wheels, the overgrowth of grasses and weeds surrounding them.

Caitlin felt grateful that the community group had provided their approximate location in order for walkers to avoid them. And here she and Nathan were, homing in.

"So, who are we looking for?" she asked, wanting to refresh both of their memories as they got closer, and also, she thought, some quiet discussion might ease the tension.

"According to the messages, it's a tall, big guy with matted, brown hair and an aggressive demeanor. Wearing a dark coat."

"Like that's helpful," Caitlin said, scanning the very dark surroundings into which a dark coat would blend in perfectly.

Nathan snorted, and she felt glad to have relieved some of the tension they were both feeling.

"He seems to have set up some kind of camp near the railway cars, but I'm not sure what it is. I don't think anyone's been up here since then. From what I read on the way here, I believe the police have inspected the area a couple of times, following up on that incident, but he hasn't been around."

"What do you think we should be looking for? A makeshift tent, a fire?"

"At this hour, a fire seems likely," Caitlin agreed, shivering. She breathed in, hoping to pick up the smell of wood smoke that might lead them to this aggressive man's lair.

She was particularly intrigued by the fact he'd used a steel bar to assault the railway engineer. A steel bar like that, if it had been used repeatedly on other victims, might contain important DNA. It might just allow them to solve the crime.

They reached the area where the abandoned railway cars had been dumped, their boots treading over wet leaves and muddy grass.

The cars were old, worn, and dirty. Some looked like they'd been there for decades.

Caitlin looked carefully, shining her flashlight around each of the cars, looking for any sign of a tent or a sleeping bag, any smells of wood smoke or cooking food, any glimpse of movement.

It worried her that if this man was ultra-aggressive, their first sighting of him might be as he leaped out to attack them with that iron bar. Her spine felt prickly, and she couldn't help feeling exposed.

"I don't see anything, do you?" Nathan whispered.

"No, nothing yet," she replied, trying to keep her breathing quiet and her movements controlled. She couldn't afford to get into the mindset of expecting an attack.

From somewhere in the distance, she heard the click-clack of a train on the tracks, and the dull blare of a whistle. From close up, something rustled to her left, and she jumped, swinging the flashlight beam around, but it was only a tree branch, caught in a flurry of wind.

She could hear the distant clanking of wheels on tracks, and the drifts of wind through the trees, and she could smell the dirt and the trees and the damp grass, but there was no hint of smoke or fire, no sight or sound of someone living in these cars.

The steel of the cars was solid and cold. The tiny scuttle of an insect was the only unusual sound.

And then, in the distance, she saw something.

"Look!" she hissed, pointing, adrenaline now rushing through her veins.

In the distance, only just visible in the flashlight's beam, was a pale shape that she felt sure must be a tent.

Slowly, steadily, they crept forward.

They reached the cars, which obstructed the view of the tent, and Caitlin felt exposed. She didn't like the idea of approaching it from their side, but they had no choice.

They both moved closer, moving carefully and quietly, scarcely able to believe their luck as they approached it. Her eyes scanned the area, looking for the tall, big, aggressive man.

It was lighter out here, and they could see the tent better. It was a small one, its material pale green, its shape boxy.

Caitlin felt the hairs on the back of her neck rise, and she stepped forward, then stopped. There was no movement and no sound coming from it. She couldn't see any light or any trace of a fire.

She and Nathan walked forward, and Caitlin breathed out slowly as they passed the last of the abandoned cars. Wherever he was, he wasn't here. She sensed no human presence nearby, heard nothing.

They reached the tent, and Caitlin shone her flashlight inside the partially open flap, but it was empty. Except for a sleeping bag in one corner and a backpack on the floor, it was empty.

"Look," Nathan said.

She swung around.

In the muddy ground a few yards from the tent, there were footprints. Large, booted footprints, clear in the mud, leading off in the direction of the track.

This was where he'd gone, and where they needed to follow.

"Let's go," she whispered, and they followed the footprints, straining to hear any sound of a voice or the movement of someone. They led down the hill to a set of old, rusted railway tracks, which they crossed. Caitlin walked carefully, as did Nathan, both of them utterly focused, shining their lights to keep the tracks in view, because when the mud was thinner, they were less visible, and they occasionally disappeared completely.

She walked a few yards behind Nathan, and in the distance, she heard something. A slight rustling in the undergrowth—the sound of someone walking softly through the bushes that clustered in the valley.

She stopped, and Nathan turned back, his face a mask of concentration.

"Did you hear that?" he whispered. "There's someone there."

"Yes," she said, her heart racing.

The rustling stopped, and they walked on, straining to hear it again.

Caitlin walked slowly, looking around. The long grasses on either side of her moved in the breeze, but she saw no sign of the person she was sure had just been in here. She shone the flashlight in a wider arc, hoping to pick up something more. The light didn't help her, but her ears did. The footsteps again, softer this time, and to her right.

She turned and saw the pale shape of someone ducking down behind the thick undergrowth.

A man, tall, big, and wearing a dark coat. It was their suspect; it had to be him. He'd been trying to get away silently, but they had been catching up. Now, he froze, staring at them, his demeanor in the dim light reminding her of a cornered animal.

"Police!" Caitlin called. "Come out, please. We need to speak to you."

She waited, holding her breath.

For a tense, long moment, there wasn't a sound to be heard.

And then, a crash of undergrowth and a stamp of boots broke the silence. Caitlin tensed, following the sound, but the noise soon told her that this suspect wasn't waiting around, and he wasn't cooperating.

He was on the run, plunging into the trees, with a speed born of panic.

"Catch him," Caitlin shouted and then she launched herself into the chase.

CHAPTER FOURTEEN

The flashlight beam bounced and jolted, casting sharp shadows over the uneven ground. This drifter, this fugitive, was running, and Caitlin knew that every moment counted in the chase.

"Stop!" she yelled. "Police!"

There was no response apart from the pounding of footsteps as he fled. He was heading for the woods, for the tall, deep bank of trees ahead, and she was terrified that if he reached them, he would get away, or else, be able to hide.

Beside her, Nathan charged forward. "We need to ask you questions," he yelled, but the drifter ignored the words.

He was going to attempt an escape. Of course he was. He had attacked a railway engineer. He'd committed one crime that they knew of and maybe more. Now they'd surprised him. He was clearly careful and sneaky and one of those who avoided the police at all costs.

She dashed through the gloom, her heart racing, and her breath burning in her lungs.

She kept her flashlight trained on where she'd seen him, but in the darkened overgrowth, it was more of a pursuit by sound than sight. Even so, she ran as fast as she could, her boots kicking up choking mud.

The rough track they were on was sloping downward, and he was picking up speed, his height and weight giving him the edge on this downhill run where all he had to do was catapult himself down the slope. The trees were coming closer and closer, and she knew that if they didn't stop him, he would reach them, and once he was hidden in the forest, it would make it much more difficult. And dangerous.

She could hear Nathan immediately behind her, his footfalls steady, running with strength and purpose.

She skidded down the slope, and then charged toward the trees, holding her flashlight high. The drifter was just ahead, and he was slowing down now, pausing, as if considering his options. She wondered if he was panicking, realizing that capture was inevitable.

There was a moment when she was certain that they were going to catch him, and that she was going to be able to grab him and put the cuffs on him.

But then, under her feet, a hidden indentation in the ground caused her to stumble badly. She nearly went sprawling onto the stony ground. With a huge effort, her ankle throbbing, she righted herself, limping forward, gritting her teeth in pain, but that small delay had given him the lead he needed.

Her stomach plummeted as she saw him disappearing into the darkness ahead, heading for the trees.

"Damn it," she said breathlessly, getting her speed up again. "He was right there."

"Are you okay?" Nathan had caught up with her.

"I'm okay." Doggedly, she tried to conceal the limp and the pain.

"We'll get him," Nathan promised. He was forging ahead of her now, and they were reaching the tree line.

The worst had happened, and their fugitive was now in the forest. Caitlin's hopes sank, but she wasn't letting herself give up. They could still catch him, and they must.

She knew that there were no guarantees when it came to tracking someone in a dark, cluttered area, whether it was a forest or a warehouse or a pitch-black factory. You could stay on their trail, or you could lose it, and there were always plenty of hiding places. She silently cursed that uneven ground that had claimed her balance and speed.

A few seconds more, and she would have had him.

Ahead of her, she could hear the thudding of Nathan's footsteps. He'd slowed down, she knew, and he was trying to be quiet, trying to listen. He was still following the drifter's trail.

Caitlin jogged forward, letting the pain in her ankle ease, her flashlight beam sweeping through the trees, trying to find any sign of the drifter. Her heart was pounding, and she was breathing as if she'd run a marathon.

She stopped for a moment, listening. The sounds of the forest were all around her: the rustle of leaves and branches, the incessant sound of insects, the occasional scuttling sound of an animal. She held her breath and listened, trying to gauge which way he'd gone.

That way. Her flashlight picked up a trodden track.

“There,” she gasped, pointing the beam so that Nathan veered in the same direction.

She took a breath and began to run again, following the trail of disturbed undergrowth. The ground was uneven and slippery, and she was very aware of the fact that she might trip again.

Even so, Caitlin pushed forward, branches whipping at her face and arms. She threw herself into the chase, knowing that if she stopped, she was going to lose her chance.

And then, there was a flash of movement up ahead. There he was!

She screamed out to him, "Stop!" at exactly the same time as Nathan. This man was closer than she'd thought. She wondered if he had been trying to hide, or catch his breath for a moment, not realizing they had tracked the footprints he'd left.

Now, he was running, speeding up for all he was worth, but he was clearly tiring.

Caitlin dashed forward, her feet flying over the uneven ground. She felt her breath gasping in her throat and the sound of her own heartbeat in her ears. She kept her pace and rhythm, trying to bypass the obstacles, the rocks, the bushes in her path, and the hidden holes and dips. All while ignoring the pain in her ankle, the stitch in her side, and the burning in her chest. This was the chase, she knew. This was what it was all about.

She was hearing him, too, now. She could hear his footfalls, the cracking of branches, the snapping of twigs, the occasional gasped swear word. She was gaining on him.

He was right there, just ahead of her. Triumph surged inside her as she realized she could see his ragged, black jeans, the coat flapping open, and his dark hair.

Nathan would get him, she realized. Nathan, a few yards ahead and powering forward, would be the one to do this takedown. But she'd be there to provide backup, to make sure that this fleeing fugitive was held.

And then, catastrophe. Another hidden hole claimed Nathan, and he went sprawling down on one knee.

Gasping in a breath, Caitlin put on speed, pounding along the narrow, uneven track that was winding between the trees. She twisted to avoid Nathan, who was scrambling to his feet, and lunged forward, making up the distance with an effort that seemed to take everything out of her.

She could see him in her flashlight beam, just ahead of her, and he was looking back, panic in his eyes. Caitlin was pumped up and determined, and she was going to make sure that he didn't get away.

She was only a few steps behind, and she was ready to dive and tackle him. Gritting her teeth, she got ready to take the plunge, and she leaped forward, closing her hands around that flapping jacket, knowing that this man was not afraid to use violence, that he'd attacked another man recently, and that she needed to contain the threat as soon as she could.

Her hands closed around the jacket. She twisted and pulled, hard, reaching to grab his arm, turning him hard, bringing him off balance as she fought to stop him.

“Hey, you bitch! Let me go! What are you doing?” He yelled in his rage, breathless and furious.

She managed to spin him around and could feel him struggling, trying to break free, but she held onto him, forcing him toward a tree, yanking his arm behind him. He tried to yank it away again, but Caitlin held on for all she was worth. She pulled the arm behind him. He was trying to turn, and she knew for sure that if he faced her, he'd attack, he'd use his fists, or he'd try to beat his way out of the situation he'd found himself in.

She pushed him up against the tree trunk, hard, twisting him away again. And then, Nathan was there, rushing up to grab his other arm.

In a moment, the handcuffs were on. Finally, she could take a look at this tall, bulky man with a bushy, brown beard. He smelled of sweat and dirt, and there was an aggressive gleam in his blue eyes that she didn't like the look of.

"What the hell you doing? What you doing to me?" he gasped, sounding irate.

"You were asked to stop. You didn't. We need to question you."

"I've got no answers to give. I hate the police," he shot back.

"That's a shame, because if you've got no answers, you'll be spending a lot of time with us. More than you wanted to," Nathan threatened breathlessly, spinning the man around.

"I don't talk to police, and I never will," he promised with a snarl.

Perhaps, Caitlin thought, there was a reason for that. They might just have captured the killer. Whatever it took, she was going to make him talk, and fast.

CHAPTER FIFTEEN

They needed answers and needed them now. Caitlin felt determined as they arrived at the police station, with their suspect sitting in angry silence in the back seat. Whenever she turned around to check on this drifter, he gave her a look through his narrowed eyes that would have scorched steel.

The local police department in Clearwell was a shoebox sized building, crammed in between a grocery store and a veterinarian's rooms. Opposite the road was the local church, a pretty building with a tall spire, which looked to be the largest and busiest of all the establishments in this small town.

They half dragged the reluctant suspect out of the car and took him inside.

"Railway task force," Caitlin introduced herself to the officer at the desk, who nodded, clearly briefed on their presence in town. "Can we use one of your interview rooms?"

"We only have one. You're welcome to use it." The officer hurried down the corridor and pulled open a door at the end, turning on the light. "Let me just organize a recording device for you and make sure it's hooked up."

It was clear this room wasn't often used for serious crimes. While he got the room prepared, Caitlin and Nathan quickly processed the man, fingerprinted him, and took what details they could. They reached a sticking point almost immediately when he refused to give his name.

"We need it for the records," Caitlin insisted, but he shook his bushy, wild-haired head.

"In that case, we'll fingerprint you and see if there's anything linked," Nathan said.

He took the fingerprints and immediately passed them to the officer who'd returned from preparing the room.

"Please let us know if there's a match for these," he said. "It's urgent as our suspect is refusing to give us his ID."

"Oh, shut up," the drifter snarled. "I have my rights."

"I'll check them straight away," the young, keen-looking officer replied, clearly pleased to have a critical job to do in this quiet police station.

They walked the suspect through to the room and sat their reluctant customer down in a chair.

He scowled at them. In the harsh light, Caitlin could see that his face was grimy with dirt, his fingernails were caked with it, and the stench coming off him was a mix of sweaty clothing and stale alcohol.

The officer returned and placed a small tape recorder on the table. "I'll leave you to it. If you need anything, just press this buzzer."

"Thanks," Caitlin said and waited until he had gone before she spoke.

"Are you going to identify yourself to us?" she asked.

The man's response was a grunt.

"You are a suspect in a murder case," Caitlin explained patiently, even though she was all out of patience with this uncooperative and aggressive man. "We need information from you. If you are innocent, then you need to work with us and clear yourself. Otherwise, we're going to have to hold you here overnight, or even longer."

"I'm not talking to the police. I hate you people. You're all corrupt. All you care about is money, giving us fines, taking bribes. Don't think I don't know that. You think we're stupid, that we'll just confess and take the fall to make you look good, but we're not! We'll fight. We'll fight for what is ours. And I won't bribe you!"

There was a complete, glaring lack of logic in that entire diatribe.

"We need to check your alibi and find out where you were at certain times." Nathan crossed his arms. "Your ID will also be important, in case you're wanted for other crimes. We heard that someone fitting your description assaulted a railway engineer recently."

"I never did that! You're just trying to frame me."

Caitlin could feel her frustration rising, but she tried to keep her own voice as composed as possible.

"Look," she said, leaning toward the man. "We're here to investigate a murder. You have been identified as a possible suspect. You need to tell us where you were on the night of the murder. You have two choices, because there are two nights where a suspect was taken. If we name the days, we need you to account for your movements."

He still said nothing. Then his face darkened, and his eyes narrowed. "You think I'm guilty, don't you? You've got me pegged for the murderer."

"If you're not giving us an alternative version, we don't really have a choice," Nathan explained. "What were you doing yesterday evening?" That was when Audrey Carter, the second victim, had disappeared and would be the easier timeline to match up.

"I was there," he grunted. "Where I live."

Caitlin shared a quick glance with Nathan. It seemed to her that this was another suspect who preferred to speak to men. They'd experienced this on their first case also. He was definitely giving answers to Nathan more easily than he'd done to her. In fact, she thought it went further than that. He was showing how much he disliked and resented being chased down and questioned by a woman by visibly cooperating with the man of the partnership.

"Alone?" Nathan asked, while Caitlin fidgeted inwardly.

"Yes," the man replied. "I live alone. I don't like many people."

"Anyone come past, greet you, ask you to move? Were you seen by anyone at all?"

"No one came to visit me," he said. "Nobody harassed me."

"Do you have a car?" Nathan asked. "How do you get around?"

"I can borrow a car when I need one," he said. "I have a connection who lives near here. He has a few old cars in his backyard. We hunt together sometimes. I want a car, I take one. I don't have to ask. Rule is, I bring it back, and I wash the cars and tend the yard to pay for it."

"You take any cars yesterday?"

"I got no need for that yesterday."

At that moment, there was a tap on the door.

Quickly, seeing Nathan had a fragile rapport and was at least getting answers out of this suspect, Caitlin went to the door.

It was the police officer who had been following up on the fingerprint checks. She stepped out to get this information without the suspect knowing about it.

Sure enough, the officer looked excited, and he held a printed page in his hand.

"This man's name is Ryan Rogers, and he has a record."

"What's it for?" Caitlin asked, glancing down at the page.

"He's been arrested in the past for robbery and for assault," the officer replied. "He was a very uncooperative prisoner, according to the report I pulled up. He was inside for a year, and during that time, he got into fights with other convicts, and he hit one of them over the head with a chair."

Caitlin nodded. "Thanks," she said.

She had reached a conclusion about this suspect, not based on the criminal record, but more based on what she'd observed while watching him in that room. She had a feeling Nathan wouldn't like her conclusion. In fact, Caitlin strongly suspected he was going to fight with her over it.

She opened the door again and beckoned to Nathan, who quickly left the room, and Caitlin told him what she'd discovered. "Ryan Rogers is our man in there. He has a record and was abusive to fellow prisoners, including hitting them over the head."

"We can confront him with that. And also, I want to go and search his tent, look for any of that nylon rope," Nathan said.

Caitlin shook her head. In a stage whisper, she argued with him. "We can do that, but I don't think he's our guy," she said.

Nathan stared at her incredulously. "What do you mean? Why? We've just established he's violent, he's aggressive, he hits people over the head, he has access to a car when he needs one, and he was in the right area at the right time." He counted the points off on his fingers, using his whole hand by the end.

"It's nothing to do with the evidence, it's more to do with who he is. I feel he's too unbalanced mentally. He's too socially awkward. Can you really see him tracking a victim down, following someone, setting up all the steps to abducting them?"

Nathan's lips tightened in a stubborn line. "Yes, I can! He's exactly the type of person we had problems with when I worked as a railway cop. That violence and aggression gets vented randomly."

"Murder-level problems?" Caitlin quirked a disbelieving eyebrow. "You had that regularly with these kinds of aggressive people? Or was it more just things like breaking into property, illegal fires, that kind of thing."

"I've had serious crimes to handle."

"So not murder?"

"Geez!" Nathan just about stamped his foot. "Anyone can escalate to murder! Why are you being like this? It's not like he's got an alibi, and he's got a record."

"I don't think he has the capacity to kill in this way. To kill, yes, but not in this way."

They glared at each other.

“What’s your alternative plan?” Nathan asked, in a way that told her he knew she didn’t have one.

Then Caitlin sighed. "I don’t have one yet. But one way or the other, we'll need to wait until it's light before we search that area for clues. What we could do is ask the local police to check inside those boxcars to make sure there are no bodies or no contraband hidden inside.”

“Yes, I guess doing it in the dark would be pointless,” Nathan agreed. At least they were agreeing on something.

“So, I guess we hold him overnight. We send local police out to check the obvious hiding places. Then tomorrow, we can get forensics to comb the area, look in his tent, get a warrant if we need one, and then question him again and confront him with the evidence."

“Yeah, we can book into a motel for tonight. There’s one at the end of this street. We can start again first thing tomorrow.”

“Maybe he’ll be more cooperative by then,” Caitlin said, trying her best to compromise and agree despite her gut feeling about him.

But she felt deeply uneasy that worse was to follow with this case, and soon. She had tried her best to get into this killer’s mind, and she had concluded that the man they were looking for was different, more methodical, more driven than this drifter was. She feared he was still out there, and she was afraid—very afraid—that the one thing that would clear Ryan Rogers was if news of a new murder came in.

Caitlin was dreading it. Worse still, she was expecting it.

These kills weren't over.

CHAPTER SIXTEEN

It was only when Caitlin had reached the motel where they were staying for the night that she realized, with a shock, that she hadn't heard back from Mike. Not since that strange text he'd sent through earlier.

What was going on with her boyfriend?

With a cold feeling, she wondered if he was really having second thoughts about this move. Holding her room key, hurrying through the nighttime drizzle toward the first-floor room she'd been assigned, she tried to call him.

It just rang. He didn't pick up, and that made her feel even more anxious. Scenarios were flooding her mind as she listened to the ringing. Was he okay? What had gone wrong? Why hadn't he updated her on the day, and his activities, and if he'd made any decisions about where to work, or schools he'd liked. There was a lot he had needed to do and hearing about it had been something she'd been looking forward to, a beam of light in a dark day.

Now, her naturally suspicious mind meant there were other scenarios going through her head, too, ones that she didn't want to think about at all as she walked down the corridor of the red brick motel, with a view of the forest, old-fashioned door keys, and planters outside each room.

Then she remembered Mike had said something about an appointment, that dinner engagement he'd had to head back to Atlanta for. She felt a rush of relief that there was a reason. But it still wasn't quite enough relief to completely quash her worry. She had questions, more of them.

She left a voice message. "Hi, Mike. How did your day go? Are you back in Atlanta safely? Let me know! Speak soon!"

Juggling her phone, bag, and key, she started opening the door to her room and then realized that, behind her, Nathan was calling her name.

She got the key in the door, turned.

"Hey, Caitlin," he called. "I just heard back from the team who went out to search that area. They said it's clean. They looked in the abandoned cars, took a walk around, called. Nothing and nobody to be seen."

"That's good, I guess," she said. Good, but not good, because rescuing a captive victim would have been first prize.

"You hungry?" Nathan asked.

She hadn't been until that moment.

"Yes," she said, surprised.

"There's a diner across the road. Shall we go there?"

"I don't—" she began, and then stopped herself.

She really did not feel like sitting down for dinner with Nathan. Not when this case was hanging over her like a lead weight, and she was now seriously worried about the future of her relationship with Mike, and when Nathan had just refused to see her point on their suspect not being the killer!

But Caitlin reminded herself sternly that this was no time to pursue an argument. She and Nathan needed to be a unit, a cohesive, cooperative pair. And that meant doing some team building. It wasn't like she had anything else to do tonight, with the case stalled. They didn't even have to discuss the case, although she was feeling obsessed by it, and planned to review all her notes later. But for an hour, they could actually act like normal humans and eat a meal. Hopefully without fighting.

"Okay, that's a good idea," she told him. "Let's have dinner."

Quickly, she dumped her bag in her room. Then, crossing the road, they went into the rustic diner.

It was packed with a mix of what looked to be mainly locals, although she picked up a couple of foreign accents, and the atmosphere was warm and happy. There was a crackling fire at one end of the room, and a wooden bar counter stretching all the way across the other.

Nathan grabbed a table somewhere in the middle, and they sat down.

As soon as she was seated, her cell phone rang. It was Mike, and she let out a quiet sigh of relief. She picked up the call immediately.

"Hey, Caitlin." Mike sounded his usual cheerful self, as if nothing at all was wrong.

"Mike," she said. "I've been looking forward to catching up. How did your day go? Did you find anything you liked, any opportunities?"

Aware she was now being rude, Caitlin mouthed "Sorry" at Nathan, who was paging through the menu in the polite way that people did when they didn't want to eavesdrop on a personal call.

"I had a look around," Mike said, "but I didn't really find anything I liked. I'm not happy with the ethos of the schools I looked at. You know, I didn't realize until now how fussy I am."

"Well, I guess there are more opportunities out there," she said, feeling dashed all the same.

"I'm going to go check out some other ones online and see if there's something that suits me better. I can't really make a decision without being sure, can I?"

"No, of course not."

"Plus, you'll probably find this funny," he said, in a hearty tone that clued Caitlin, from experience, that she would not in fact find it funny.

"What?" she asked.

"The school I'm at has an opening for vice principal, and they've asked me to put my resume in for it."

"Oh," Caitlin said, feeling as if she'd had cold water sluiced down her back.

"So, I guess I have some big decisions to make."

It didn't seem like she was a meaningful part of any of these decisions. That was Caitlin's take-home right now, and it was hurting her big time.

"I guess you do," she said coldly. "So, I'll leave you to make them, I'm with my work colleague and am being rude by taking a personal call."

"Okay. Speak later." He sounded cheery, as if he hadn't even heard the cold and annoyed note in her voice. Caitlin cut the call with a sigh.

"Sorry," she said again to Nathan, hurriedly looking at the menu. The waitress was hovering. Quickly, she ordered the grilled chicken and a side salad. Nathan went for the double cheeseburger. They each ordered a beer.

"Everything okay at home?" Nathan asked when the waitress left. Caitlin guessed his menu reading hadn't prevented him overhearing that conversation.

Caitlin sighed. "Getting Mike to relocate is not as simple as I thought it would be," she said.

"Why? What's the problem?"

"It's—everything. I think deep down, he has changed his mind and wants to stay in Atlanta, for now, at any rate. None of the schools here seem good enough. He's been offered an opportunity over there, and I think he likes it better. So, I'd better get used to a long-distance relationship until he comes around to the idea. If he ever does," she said with a grimace.

"I'm sorry," Nathan said, frowning in concern. Caitlin was touched and surprised to hear real sympathy in his tone. "That's not easy. I saw how much you were looking forward to having him move here."

She'd never thought of Nathan as an empathetic person. In fact, she hadn't even realized he was paying attention to Caitlin's personal life, the times she'd briefly mentioned it. Clearly, he was, and he had been.

The beers arrived, and Caitlin took a long swallow. After the day she'd had, she needed it.

"I guess he's a person who needs time to think about things, but I thought he was really excited about it."

She'd been happy and contented in their relationship and wanting more. She knew she was ready for the next step, to work toward a full commitment, even marriage, but maybe he wasn't at that stage, and that was why it was feeling as if they were spinning their wheels.

"Maybe he's being too fussy," Nathan said, surprising her with his critical tone. "I mean, there's nothing wrong with the schools here, is there?"

Was he implying the fault lay with Mike? Caitlin thought he might be doing that, without wanting to actually say it.

"I'm hoping he starts seeing this move in a better light, because I don't think he's doing that now," she admitted.

"I guess you have to keep on pushing for it, then," Nathan said. "I agree though, it's not nice to have to pressure someone into a decision like that when it should come from them."

Caitlin sighed. "I know. It feels awkward," she said. "Anyway, enough about that. Tell me about your situation. Do you have anyone special in your life?"

She hadn't asked him about that. It had felt as if it was prying to ask personal questions when their entire working relationship was so new, and there had been so much else to focus on. Now, she was wondering if he'd also had personal upheaval with the move to Kansas City. She felt strangely shy to ask. She wasn't good at asking other people about themselves. Perhaps that was because she was fairly private herself.

Nathan shook his head. "I haven't had much time for relationships recently," he said.

"Why's that?" Interested, now, Caitlin decided to take it further.

"I had a bad break up a while ago."

"I'm sorry," she sympathized, hearing the pain in his voice.

He shrugged. "Since then, I've been so focused on work that I haven't had time for anything else. But I guess it's time to start getting back into the dating game, especially if we're settling in this new city."

"Yes, I guess this would be a good time to do it," Caitlin agreed.

"I do love being with someone special. My ex and I had some great times together. Unfortunately, when things go wrong, and your heart's involved, they always seem to be destructive. Never mind getting back in the game, it feels like getting back into the boxing ring!" He quirked an eyebrow at her.

Caitlin laughed but couldn't help feeling a twinge of unease. Would she be heading for a few rounds in that same boxing ring sooner than she'd thought?

The waitress brought over their food, and they both ate in silence for a few minutes. While she enjoyed her food, Caitlin thought again about the case. It wasn't easy to go an hour without worrying about it.

It was thinking about what the following day might bring and needing to search through the drifter's tent and belongings, that got Caitlin wondering about a common factor she had not yet considered.

Was there something that these dumpsites had in common? There was something that was occurring to her, at the back of her mind, from the crime scene photos and from the scene she had personally attended.

Both the victims were dumped at junctions, she realized. Was that a coincidence? Or was he choosing that for a reason? Was it somehow significant for him?

Caitlin thought that was important. It might even be the first window into the killer's modus operandi that they'd had.

Or maybe, she decided, it was a window into his thinking, and a way to find him.

The idea was still too tenuous in her mind to tell Nathan, who in any case believed they had the killer in custody. But first thing in the morning, she decided, she was going to map those junctions out. There might be a pattern forming, and if so, she needed to get ahead of the murderer. Predicting this pattern might mean saving a life.

CHAPTER SEVENTEEN

It was almost time to do his work again, Mr. Last Chance thought, and he had the perfect subject in mind for his next interrogation. He'd just dumped the body of the last man he killed. Perhaps they would find it tomorrow. He didn't think they'd pick it up tonight, not in the dark place he'd chosen.

He was about to make another move, and he was going to make it now—tonight.

A dark thrill coursed through him at the thought, but he justified the thrill by thinking of the importance of his work.

If only people would understand the weight of their decisions, and the impact that they had.

After all, he, too, had suffered that way. What he was doing was simply giving others the benefit of what he himself had learned.

"It seems like years, but it's only been a few months," he said in tones of surprise, as he opened the refrigerator. He'd intended to take out a beer, for some sustenance and hydration before heading out, but to his surprise, he found his attention distracted by the photos inside the magnetic frames on the door.

A smiling woman with smooth, dark hair in a ponytail, a face that was broad and pleasant and good natured. A young boy staring shyly at the camera. An older woman, her face lined and wise.

He'd known them all back in another time, another place, before he had made the reckless choice to change their lives for the better. Ha! How misguided, how foolhardy that had been. How murderous, in fact.

"You see how wrong that was?" he told himself in stern, warning tones. "What a bad mistake you made! And others want to do the same? No, no, no, not any longer. Definitely not on my watch!"

He shook himself as if shaking away those memories, took out a beer, popped the lid, and took a long drink. It tasted flat, but it was cold and wet, and that was what counted.

It was time to get ready. He had a job to do, and he had to keep himself in shape for it. He had no choice. If he didn't do his part, then he served no purpose.

"If only they would appreciate the lesson I'm teaching them," he murmured to himself.

He turned away from the refrigerator, headed out of the kitchen, and got into his car. This man that he was going to see next drank and socialized in the evenings, in a bar that just happened to be close to where Mr. Last Chance's current abode was. Just a few blocks away, in fact.

He drove through the night, easing the car along, not wanting to attract any attention to himself. Luckily, he was one of those who enjoyed the journey as much as the destination. He smiled as he completed the leisurely drive.

It wasn't long before he was parking on the side of the road and walking toward the bar. There were a few people there; it was a small neighborhood setup, with a couple of outside tables that at this time of the year were never used and a few more inside, where he could hear music was playing.

The street was quiet. Most people were already wrapped up with their families and their television sets. There was little traffic.

He eased his car down the road, and as he did, he thought about what was ahead. This man deserved to understand the seriousness of the choices he made, at least. It wasn't his fault that he didn't.

He parked the car a little away from the bar and got out. He'd been here before, and he knew that there was a back entrance leading out of the bar. A short driveway led to a secluded parking area, and that was where he had seen this man liked to keep his car. He headed in that direction, and as he did, he made sure that he was carrying his weapon—the heavy, wooden stick felt smooth and weighty in his hand.

He wanted to be prepared.

He took a few steps along the alley and then he paused. He could see the back of the bar, and there was the door he was looking for.

This man played pool in the evenings, and after his pool games, he'd leave by this entrance. Personally, Mr. Last Chance thought that was to avoid any cops who might or might not be watching this bar, as he suspected that the man might be over the limit when he drove home.

But home wasn't far, and who was he to criticize that choice? He didn't try to micromanage every aspect of people's lives. No, no, it was another choice that he wanted to quiz this man about today. Or rather, tonight.

He waited. He had patience. He knew that this man would come this way.

Then he heard the footsteps. A few moments later, the door opened and out stepped the man he was looking for. He didn't look drunk, Mr. Last Chance had to admit. He looked happy and was whistling to himself, shrugging on his jacket as he headed for the parking lot.

Quickly, he stepped into the shadows and out of sight. He felt an adrenaline rush, a burst of excitement at what he was going to do. He had never realized, when he began this very important work, that he would savor these moments. After all, they were extremely action filled, and it seemed that at his heart, he was a lover of action.

He couldn't wait for events to unfold now. Although he knew this was going to be a moment that seemed to pass in a flash, he'd replay it to himself again and again when he thought about it, once safely back home.

This was the exciting part, the time when he still had hope for the people he took. He was invested in their decisions and rooting for them to make the best one. It was a pity most people made the worst. After that happened, he always felt sad and filled with regret as he laid their bodies out on the rails. In fact, he shed a tear sometimes, but that was not only from sadness, but also from relief that they wouldn't have to suffer the consequences of their terrible decision.

Mr. Last Chance stepped forward, one hand behind his back, where his weapon was concealed. He couldn't see the car, but he knew that the man would be walking along the sidewalk and turning right to get to it. He would be a couple of steps away from where Mr. Last Chance was standing, and he'd never know that he was there.

Here he was, approaching briskly, his feet scrunching over the ground.

Crouching lower, feeling his heart pounding hard, Mr. Last Chance made sure to keep absolutely still, to become invisible.

As the man passed, Mr. Last Chance straightened. It was time to give this man a chance to do the right thing. It was time to give him a chance to understand the true impact of his choice.

He grabbed the weapon and broke into a run. He loved this moment. Preparing, tensing himself, checking that the coast was clear, and then bringing down his weapon with exactly the right amount of force. Not too much, that was imperative. He only wanted to stun the man for as long as it took.

The thud as the stick hit his head was satisfying, as was the way he stumbled and collapsed to his knees.

Perfectly subdued. This might be his finest display of judgment and coordination yet. What an art he was creating.

With a grunt of effort, Mr. Last Chance threw the man over his shoulder in a fireman's lift. Then he strode back to his car, opened the spacious trunk, and placed the man carefully inside. He never tossed his victims like a sack. That would be wrong. If this man was making the right choice, he didn't deserve to be battered or bruised.

Quickly, expertly, he secured his hands behind him and his ankles, too, just to be sure. No need to take any risks here. He couldn't afford to.

Then he got into his car and started it up, driving calmly out of town to the place he had identified, an old junction on a part of the track that ran through deep woods, but with significance to it about what was nearby. He drove smoothly, taking his time, making sure that the man was secure in the trunk.

As he drove away, he knew he had done the right thing. This was what it took to make a man understand his actions, to make him realize just how wrong they really could be.

"I have some questions for you," he told the man, who of course couldn't hear him, but that didn't matter because it was fun to prepare, to ready himself. "I can't wait for the answers," he muttered, and to his surprise, a tight smile spread over his face.

This man would have a chance, after all. They all did.

But would he take it?

CHAPTER EIGHTEEN

Caitlin woke in the morning, while it was still dark, jolted from sleep by her theory of patterns. She had been dreaming about railroad tracks, crisscrossing in a series of junctions. She wanted to explore that idea further, but before she could do that, her phone started ringing.

She stared at it suspiciously, seeing it was Aniyah calling, and knowing that an early call like this was more than likely bad news. Not wanting to delay the news a moment longer, she quickly picked up. "Morning, Aniyah. What's up?" she said.

"This isn't good, Caitlin," Aniyah said, and Caitlin was grateful for her forthrightness. She wasn't wasting any time. "Another victim has been found. I just got the details. Sketchy, but I have the location at least."

The news hit Caitlin like an actual blow. She let herself absorb the shock for a moment. Then, she asked the important question. "Where?"

The priority now was to rush to the scene.

"I'm going to send you the coordinates. It looks to be a few miles from the other scenes, further west, but definitely in the same area."

"Thanks," Caitlin said. She was already scrambling out of bed, flinging on her clothes, and packing up the few items that weren't already in her bag.

"I'll call Nathan now," Aniyah promised.

Caitlin rushed out of the motel room and headed to the lobby. As she got there, Nathan arrived, with his hair in disarray and still pulling on his jacket.

"Another one?" he asked. "This seems impossible."

Caitlin nodded, feeling hollow. They needed so many answers, but Aniyah had done the right thing by calling them immediately. They could get more answers this way.

"Yes, I know, it seems impossible. It's just a few miles away. Let's go."

This did not necessarily rule out their suspect in custody, and she was sure Nathan was well aware of that. Only once they established the time of death could they assess whether Ryan Rogers could have killed this victim or not. It could have been an old body, recently found.

They hurried to the car and drove off, following the coordinates that Aniyah had sent, which Nathan mapped into the screen as Caitlin drove. They were doing this together, as a team. There were three of them, plus the area's police departments, fighting this criminal. But even so, Caitlin had never felt more alone or more unsure.

She drove as fast as she could, feeling that if they didn't get there as soon as they could, it would be too late.

The problem was that it was already too late. And that fact was like a shard of ice in her gut. The knowledge festered inside her as she veered off the side road, following a rutted track up into the hills.

They climbed out, looking around.

Aniyah must have heard about this crime immediately, Caitlin realized, because there was only one police car at the scene so far, and another pulled up just after they arrived.

"Morning," the officer in charge said, hurrying over to them. "Forensics and the coroner haven't yet arrived on scene, so please, can you keep away from the body until they arrive?"

"Sure," Caitlin said.

"It's about half a mile away on that gravel path."

As she'd thought, this was another inaccessible area.

"Who found the body?" she asked.

"A group of men out hiking. They are still on the scene," he said.

As Caitlin trudged over the uneven path, she realized again that this killer was carrying these victims a long way. And he knew about the tracks. This did not look like a well-used railway. This looked like abandoned infrastructure. Although, as she approached the scene, Caitlin amended her thinking. There was a new railway line, to her right, a few yards away and running parallel to the old tracks.

And ahead was the body. She stared at it, feeling angry and defeated and wishing she could somehow have turned the clock back to stop what he had done.

The wrappings had been partially undone. Clearly, the hikers had not imagined what could have been underneath, or else, had been simply curious and unaware of the recent crimes.

Peering at the deceased victim, Caitlin felt a sense of shock. Without a doubt, this was a man; she could see his short beard. Up until now, she'd guessed that he was targeting women specifically. But now, she needed to revise those parameters.

To the side, she saw three men, standing, looking shocked. They all looked to be in their sixties or even seventies, gray haired, fit looking, and warmly clad in hiking gear.

She hurried over to them. Nathan was speaking to the cops on the scene in a low voice, getting information from them to add to their arsenal.

"Good morning. Sorry about these circumstances. I'm an agent investigating this crime. You found the body?" she asked.

The closest man stepped forward. He was lean and rangy, with a shock of gray hair and wearing dark glasses.

"We found it about an hour ago, ma'am," he said. "Most shocking experience of our lives."

"It's a shame you had to go through this, and I'm grateful you called the police fast. Talk me through what happened?" Caitlin invited.

"Well, we usually hike this way, three times a week, and we always look out for anything along the way that could cause problems. When Dan here saw this bundle on the actual rails, he said we should go and look. Pete said that the rails were not in use, but in the end, we thought it would be better to check, just in case. We actually thought it was stolen goods, a stash of contraband, something like that. We were shocked when we moved the tarps and saw it was a man."

"Did you see anyone else around?"

The man shook his head. "No one. We were on our own. It was just us."

"And do you recognize the victim?" Caitlin asked.

"Actually, I might," Dan said, and the others nodded somberly in acknowledgement. "He looked a lot like the guy from the hardware store in town. I don't know his name, but he's always there when I come in to shop."

"Pierre. That's his name," another one of the men said.

"It looked like him, but I know he told me last time we spoke that he had changes ahead. Not sure if he was moving branches or what he was doing. There was a girlfriend involved, I recall."

"He hadn't moved yet," the other man insisted, and they started arguing in an amicable way. Caitlin had a strong feeling that the discussion was helping all of them release the tension and grief they'd felt on their discovery of the body.

Behind her, she heard voices, and looking around, she saw to her relief that forensics and the coroner, whom she recognized from the previous scene, had arrived.

As she waited for the coroner to do his initial exam, Caitlin looked around the scene. She saw Nathan doing the same.

"It's such an out of the way spot. How did this killer even know about it?" she asked.

"Yes. Why here? Why walk all this way?" he said, shaking his head regretfully as he stared around. She guessed that like her, he was looking for some magic bullet, some piece of evidence that might miraculously point the way. But in this grim, gray, early morning scene, she was sure that there would be nothing like that.

They would need to dig.

She walked over to the coroner, after pulling on a head cover and foot covers. "Do you have any initial findings?" she asked.

"So far, I have an approximate time of death," he said.

"And?"

"My estimation, given the level of rigor mortis and other indications, is about twelve hours ago, give or take an hour or two. This is a relatively recent scene," he said. The note of authority and confidence in his voice left no room for doubt.

And just like that, Caitlin knew, the suspect in custody was cleared. They were looking for someone different. Again, those thoughts of junctions came back to her. This time, there were three cases to refer to and not just two.

It was time to see if mapping them might give a window into the killer's logic, because he was so far ahead of them that they desperately needed to predict his next move.

CHAPTER NINETEEN

"What's your next move?"

The words resounded in Malcolm Coombes's ears like knives, assaulting him in the darkness. He felt totally confused, and as if he had a nasty bump on his head.

What had happened? Why was he here? And who was speaking?

He stifled a groan as he tried to struggle into a sitting position, but that seemed impossible. His hands were tied behind him. What in the name of all that was holy was actually going on here? The darkness was so absolute that it felt suffocating. It felt as if he'd been in this position for ages, and he was freezing cold.

He could hear birdsong somewhere. Was it very early morning? It was still dark in here, that was for sure.

But then, he gasped as a brilliant light was shone in his face, searing his retinas painfully.

He twisted away, blinking rapidly. This was not a good situation; it couldn't be. This man must have taken him, grabbed him as he was leaving the bar. That was his last memory, anyway. Leaving that bar.

"I don't … I don't understand," Malcolm said. He was shaking, now, with shock and confusion, and his mind was a total blank. He couldn't think straight.

"Your next move. That's what I've asked you about."

"But who are you?"

"Never mind that. Just give me the answer."

All he knew of his captor was this merciless-sounding voice and the inexorable glare of the light. He realized that his head was pressed up against metal. Where was he? And what on earth was going on here?

"How can I answer you when I don't understand the question?"

"I'm going to explain the question now. You can think about it if you like, but it's important."

"Okay, okay, what do you want to know?" He couldn't believe this. He'd been abducted, imprisoned, and now someone was interrogating him?

"You are planning a life change. Aren't you?"

"A life—How did you know?" he asked, feeling shocked. How had this man known that there was a change ahead for him? More to the point, why had he been abducted?

A memory was filtering back to Malcolm, a faint memory of something someone had said at the bar, he had no idea how long ago. A lifetime ago, it seemed now. But this someone had said that two local women had recently been taken and had been found murdered.

Now, with a chill, Malcolm was wondering if he was the third. Was he in the killer's clutches? He had a horrible feeling that this was the same man.

And he somehow knew, he had somehow found out, that Malcolm was planning a move. It was something he was excited about, a positive step in his life. He was going to move across the state and take up a new position at a new branch of the company that they were opening.

It was a good career move. He felt excited and motivated about it. And yet there were a lot of drawbacks too. For a start, it had meant that he would be leaving the place he'd grown up, the friends he knew. It was definitely a step out of his comfort zone.

He'd asked for some time to think about it. How on earth had this man known this? Was he a mind reader? What if someone had been following him and reporting back? Why was this decision even important to anyone else?

He swallowed. This was really, really bad.

"You're right, I am considering a change, a big change. And I don't understand how you know that."

"Considering?" There was something in his voice, in his words. "I don't believe you."

"But—"

"No. You're just playing for time. You're saying that to make me think you're not certain, so I'll give you more leeway. But you are certain. And you're just too scared to admit it."

"That's not true!"

"No? Prove it. Tell me the truth. You're moving, aren't you?"

Malcolm had the odd feeling that what he was about to say mattered a lot. That it could mean life or death, in fact. Was this man just waiting for him to say anything before killing him? Or was he going to seal his own fate if he gave a precise answer that this man didn't want to hear?

Now, he felt agonized. Was there a wrong decision?

Through his aching, hurting head, he tried his best to think. He was a local man; he'd lived in this area his whole life long. He had known one of the other victims slightly. What was her name? The insurance lady. Edna? Yes, he thought she was Edna. She'd helped him with a few different issues over the years. There had been that time his motorcycle was stolen, and also that issue he'd had with the leak in his car.

And she'd been moving, for sure. She'd actually sent out a "Dear Clients" notification, which he'd received just three days ago, to say that she was relocating next month and would not be available to assist any more clients personally. She'd given the contact number of the man who she was training up to replace her. He'd heard from someone at the bar that she was moving because she was getting divorced, but he didn't know if that was correct or not.

He would have to give a truthful answer to that question, he thought.

Or did he? Malcolm hesitated. He had a feeling that this was a potentially fatal mistake to make.

What if he just lied? Wasn't he entitled to do that?

No, he couldn't lie. This man might know more, it might make him mad. Most likely he was going to kill him anyway. He might as well just give the true answer.

Then he paused again. Was honesty really going to get him killed? He was confused, so, so hurt and exhausted. And maybe this man would just kill him regardless and get it over with.

The cold metal was digging into his back like a blade. His head was pounding. He'd never felt so miserable or so afraid in his life. He could hear the man shifting slightly, his quiet breathing behind that blazing light. Malcolm had no idea, none at all, who he was. His voice was not familiar, but then again, he wondered if he had heard it before in passing. He was definitely not someone he knew well.

He briefly considered begging for his life.

But that wouldn't work, he was sure of it. This man, if it was the same person, had killed twice before, and Malcolm was certain that he was going to laugh at the begging, and it might even work against him.

With a sudden shift of his mind, he decided that he was going to take the plunge. He was going to lie. He groaned to disguise the sudden surge of fear he felt at this renegade action.

"I was considering it very strongly, but just yesterday I emailed them to say I'm declining the offer," he said, feeling the taste of fear sharp in his mouth, and his heart was now racing. Lying might work out badly for him.

"Really? Why?"

His mind flailed, trying to think of a good reason. "In the end, I didn't want to move away from my home and my friends, and I was scared that the new job would interfere with my freedom too much. It would involve a lot of weekend work, they said, and I live for my motorcycle. I like to ride on weekends." He breathed in, then out. "Plus, the salary was higher, but when I did the math, I found out that living there would be more expensive, so it wasn't a huge increase." Now, he was getting into the rhythm of his lie, embellishing on it—but not too much, he warned himself.

"I strongly considered it, but what sealed my decision was that they also offered me a salary increase to stay here, when we started discussing numbers."

It was difficult to do, especially since he was now worried that the lie was causing him to sweat, but he smiled a weak smile that he hoped looked satisfied.

There was silence. A long, long silence. The light switched off.

And then, Malcolm felt a cloth, with a strange chemical smell, covering his face and his mouth.

It muffled the screams he tried to make as he was swallowed by darkness.

CHAPTER TWENTY

"I noticed something about all these body dumping sites," Caitlin told Nathan, as they stood in the woods, listening to the early morning birdsong, interspersed with the crackle of radios as the forensics and more police arrived on the murder scene.

"What?" he asked.

"All of them are near junctions. Either old ones, or old into new. In fact, all of them look as if they are at places where new rails have been joined with old."

"But that could just be coincidence," Nathan argued.

“This could be an important lead. And this body was dumped on abandoned tracks. Who would even know about abandoned tracks? They’re not on the map!”

Now, Nathan frowned.

"Who would know this?"

"I guess we could ask at the local railway administration office."

Nathan looked around. "We might as well head there now. I think they're going to be working here a while, and to be honest, I'll be surprised if this scene gives us anything new."

Caitlin nodded grimly. "I feel the same. I think this killer is being very careful. They'll be lucky to find anything here, and if they do, there’s no point in waiting when we can use the time better."

They headed for the car. She got in the driver's side, and Nathan got on the phone to find out where the closest railway administration office was.

It was in the neighboring town of Woodville, so they headed straight there—a short, six-mile drive through thickly wooded hills. Caitlin couldn't get the idea of those junctions out of her mind. She was sure that this must mean something important and hoped that they'd be able to find out what.

The drive passed very quickly—all the more so because she did exceed the limit, just by a few miles per hour, when she thought it was safe to do so. Despite Nathan looking meaningfully at the speedometer every time. Irritating, right?

It didn't take long to find the railway admin office. The administration office was an old, red brick building, set on a hill in the center of the town, overlooking a small marketplace.

It looked to be just opening up for the day. A woman in a blue uniform was setting out stands with brochures and straightening a poster in the window informing the public of updates and improvements to certain train lines.

"Morning," the woman said, as she looked up from her work. She had curly, gray hair, sharp, blue eyes, and a weathered face and hands that told Caitlin that some of her life, at least, had probably been spent working outdoors.

Behind her was another man, who looked to be in his fifties, working behind the glassed counter. He seemed to be filing what looked like a mountainous pile of documents.

"Morning," Caitlin said. Needing to get to the point fast. She continued, "We're from the railway task force." She showed her badge.

"Oh, goodness," the woman said, turning away from her work and looking worried. "Does this have anything to do with the train killings we've been hearing about? We have a special safety briefing on that later today."

"Yes, we're looking for information on the murder sites," Caitlin said.

"Well, I don't know anything about them, I'm afraid. I've never seen anything suspicious on the lines. I mean, I've had friends that have been robbed on their train journeys, but I've never seen any suspicious activity on the tracks."

"We noticed that all these murders have taken place near junctions," Caitlin explained.

"They have? What sort of junctions?" the woman asked, with a frown.

"The ones where rails from old lines have been joined with rails from new lines," Nathan added.

"Who would know where those were?" the woman asked, thoughtfully, as if to herself. "I don't, I'm afraid," she told them.

"Well, that's actually what we're wondering. We are looking for information on who might know this," Caitlin said. "It seems to be quite difficult to find out where certain junctions are? The most recent murder site is actually on an old, abandoned track, and you'd have to know the history or else have walked the area. So that's why we were wondering if there is anyone with expert knowledge."

"It's the first time I've been asked that question!" the woman admitted. "I'm not sure anyone working here would know. I feel you might be wasting your time," she said regretfully.

"Who would know? Any long-term employees?" Nathan suggested.

"Let me phone the office manager and ask him," she said.

"Hold on." She dialed a number and spoke to someone in a muffled voice. After a minute, she hung up.

"Sorry. He's in a meeting right now, but the safe answer would be no, no one here would know. The manager has only been here a year or so."

"The head office, then?" Nathan suggested.

"Well, this is the area's head office," she explained.

"So, he can't think of anyone else who would have details?" Nathan asked.

"No," she confirmed. "It's a real shame that I can't help."

Caitlin felt disappointed and frustrated that this lead, which she'd had high hopes for, was proving to be impossible to explore. But as she was about to thank the woman and leave, the man working behind the desk cleared his throat.

"Um, Ruth, I've just thought of someone who has got that information."

Caitlin hurried to the glassed counter.

"Which person is that?" she asked him.

He looked at her, a frown creasing his pale face, pushing his glasses up onto his high forehead.

"I'm in the archiving department, so Ruth wouldn't have known this. But a few years ago, the managers wanted to get all the tracks mapped out and get an up-to-date record on which lines were old, which were new, and where the joins were."

"They did?" Ruth asked, her voice intrigued.

"Yes, it was for costing reasons. They wanted to do a costing exercise on what they might be in for in terms of replacing the older railway tracks over the next few years."

"Well, that is interesting," Ruth said.

Caitlin thought it was interesting too. "So, you're saying there is a record?"

"Well, unfortunately not," the man said apologetically. "The contractor they hired to do the work quit the project halfway through. He was the one with the best local knowledge, and I don't think they've been able to find anyone to replace him. And they probably haven't tried, after the disaster it became."

"Why was it a disaster?" Caitlin asked.

"Well, the man himself, Todd McDermott, had … I guess you could call it a mental breakdown, a couple of months into the project. He'd been going through difficulties. I don't remember what they were. Family problems of some kind. Anyway, he then refused to do any more work."

"And did the railways try to push him to?"

"Yes, they tried. We were on the point of getting lawyers involved. He actually assaulted one of the officials in a meeting. Hit him over the head with one of the archive books. In the end, I think they just took out a restraining order against him to say he was not allowed near the offices, and they then shelved the project. As I said, it was very unpleasant." He shrugged. "I am sure he must have been unstable before that time, but sadly it was that project that pushed him over the edge. The stress, I guess."

But Caitlin now realized that in terms of leads, this was pure gold. In fact, this sounded like exactly the man they were looking for.

"I guess he's a local man? Still in town?"

"Last I heard, yes. He lived on the outskirts of town, and I think he's still around."

Caitlin exchanged an excited glance with Nathan. She knew where they were going next.

CHAPTER TWENTY ONE

Todd McDermott was not easy to track down. Right from the start, Caitlin realized, this was a slippery customer.

The address they'd been given was out of date. When they arrived at the old building that was his last recorded residence, they found it had been renovated into three new, modern offices. Feeling frustrated, Caitlin knocked on the door of the first one, which had a sign above it: Steve's Fishing Supplies.

As she waited, Nathan looked on his phone, calling up the available ID images for the man they were seeking.

"This is him," he said, showing Caitlin the picture of a hard-faced man, with a square jaw, who looked to be in his early forties. She stared at it for a few moments, cementing the picture in her mind so that she'd know him at a glance.

Then they heard footsteps, and the door was opened by a good-natured-looking man with graying hair, who was holding a fishing tackle box in his hand, clearly in the process of unpacking an order.

"Can I help you?" he asked.

"We're looking for Todd McDermott. He used to live here," Caitlin said.

"Todd? Yes, I think he sold up to the company who refurbished these offices. But I don't know where he went. I do know of him, because at one stage, he bought fishing equipment from my old shop," he said. "But he's definitely kept to himself for the last few years."

"Do you know if he had any friends nearby, any close connections who he associates with?"

"No, I'm afraid not," the man said, shaking his head. "The only person I've seen around here recently is his mother. She's been here a couple of times, to the doctor's rooms next door. I think she's the only person he really associates with. He's a bit of a loner. I've never seen him with any friends. Not since I've moved here, anyway." Suddenly, he looked as if inspiration had struck. "You know, I think I did hear that he lives with his mother now," he added, finally giving them the piece of information that they really needed.

"Great," Nathan said. "Where can we find Mrs. McDermott?"

"Four houses down," he said with a smile. “The name’s on the mailbox.”

They got back in the car and hustled there.

A minute later, Caitlin jumped out of the car again and raced up the neatly kept garden path to knock on the green-painted front door. This was turning into a race to find this man, and if he was the killer, she had no illusions that it would be a race against time to save a life.

She looked at the window, but the curtains were drawn. There didn't seem to be any activity inside. She waited a minute and then knocked on the door again. Once more, there was no answer.

"Mrs. McDermott?" Caitlin called.

And then, finally, from around the side of the house, a woman appeared, spry and gray haired, wearing a smock and gardening gloves.

"Are you Mrs. McDermott?" Caitlin asked.

"Yes?" the woman replied warily, looking them up and down.

"We're seeking information on recent crimes, and we'd like to speak to your son. Is Todd home?"

"Todd?" she said, as if she'd never heard the name.

"Yes. Todd McDermott," Caitlin repeated.

"Oh, he's not home now," she said, but she was looking evasive.

Caitlin felt a clench of fear. Not being home was never going to be a good outcome for a suspected killer. What if he was out, stalking another victim?

"When do you expect him back?" Caitlin asked.

"I don't know. He never tells me when he's going out."

"What car does he drive?" Caitlin asked.

"He has an old Ford SUV, gray," she replied.

You could easily get a body into the back of that, Caitlin reasoned.

"Do you know where he's gone?"

"No. He doesn't tell me those things, you see."

She smiled sweetly, but she was lying, Caitlin was sure of it. The way her gaze slid away was a tell.

"Listen, Mrs. McDermott, it's very important we find your son. Is he working anywhere?" Nathan asked.

"No. He doesn't work anymore."

Caitlin felt a chill of fear. "Why is that?" She kept her voice carefully controlled, trying to hide her anxiety.

"He's not well. He's ... he's trying to get himself together again. He had a breakdown, you see. He has a small trust fund payment, so he's been living at home, paying his way, while I do the cooking and cleaning."

"Is he seeing anyone? A counselor?"

"Well, yes, in the town. He's been going to see a doctor. He's been taking medication. But he don't always take it, you know. Some days he skips it."

Caitlin was still feeling uneasy. The woman was clearly lying about knowing Todd's whereabouts, and Caitlin had to find out why she was lying. If this was the man responsible for the murders, his mother was shielding him, and she needed to crack through her defenses fast.

"Mrs. McDermott, look, I'm going to be honest with you. We are dealing with serial crimes. Your son might have important information that can help us. We need to try and find him, and it's very important that we do this fast. Do you want to be responsible for another death? Because if we don't get the information, that's a risk."

She carefully did not say that this mother's son was a suspect. That was not going to open any doors, Caitlin knew. But Mrs. McDermott did look as if she was now persuaded.

"Well, I don't want to be responsible for any deaths. He might be down the road," she said reluctantly.

"Down the road where?"

"In Burt's Bar. He likes to spend some time there on the days when he's free."

Burt's Bar. They finally had a location for this suspect—if he was there.

"If we don't find him there, we'll come back and wait here," Caitlin said with a polite smile, just in case the woman was saying this just to get them off her front doorstep. But she nodded, looking more serious now as she took in the enormity of the crimes.

"You should find him there," she reassured them.

Caitlin and Nathan headed straight to the bar. It was just a few minutes down the road. The bar was at the end of a row of small shops, a dilapidated-looking building with a big, neon sign that blinked randomly, flashing green and yellow against the cloudy sky.

Dilapidated as the big brick place might look, it definitely did seem to be popular. There were about fifteen cars parked outside, and Caitlin saw two different Ford SUVs that fitted the description. Hopefully, he'd be inside. With luck, they could question him and even arrest him if they didn't get the answers that satisfied them.

Pushing the door open, Caitlin saw the place was smoky and dark, and it took a moment for her eyes to adjust as they walked through the bar room, looking around. It was a typical place, with a bar along one wall and a pool table in the far corner. The lights were low, and the place was nearly full, even at this hour of midmorning.

She looked at all the tables but didn't see him there. Where was he? At the bar itself, perhaps? There he was. She recognized the squareness of his jaw, which was distinctive even in this low light.

Quickly, she walked over to him, aware that there were already a few unfriendly glances cast in their direction. This was not a place where law enforcement was welcomed, that was obvious.

He turned, and he was just as she'd remembered him from the photo. His jaw was square, his hair was closely cropped, his eyes were intense.

"Todd McDermott?" she asked.

"Yes?" he asked, his voice deep and gruff. He didn't look scared to see police arriving. Rather, she thought, he looked aggressive, as if ready for a fight.

"We need to talk to you, Mr. McDermott," she said. "It's in connection with the recent murders."

"What? You think I've killed somebody?" he asked, surprised and outraged. The men at the bar were looking shocked. She heard angry voices rise around him.

"We need to find the killer, and you might have information that will help us do that," she said calmly. "You need to come with us." She wanted to get him out of this environment, which was feeling more and more hostile.

And Todd himself was the most hostile of all. Angrily, he jumped off the bar stool, looking ready to fight.

"I haven't done anything wrong!" he declared. "You police are nothing but bullies."

"Do you have information that could help us? It’s all we need," Caitlin asked, trying to keep him calm and reasoning.

"I'm not answering any questions," he said.

"You tell 'em," the man next to him urged.

As if spurred on by this encouragement, the man on the other side agreed. "They are just here to harass you. They are treating you like a criminal."

"What is he accused of?" another man called out. There was a chorus of shouts from behind him. Nathan turned in his direction and hurried over, clearly seeing something in that part of the bar that needed to be controlled, fast.

This was not the reaction Caitlin had hoped for. She could see other men stirring now, and angry glances were being cast at them. She saw the pool cues being taken up, and she heard the clink of bottles. This was going to go downhill fast. Was this a fight they could handle?

"You're coming with us," Caitlin said, her tone firm.

He looked totally hostile now, and she wasn't sure if this was because he was the murderer, or because they were cops.

"This is harassment!" he yelled.

And the next moment, Caitlin found herself slammed back against the table behind her by a blow that was so quick and vicious she hadn't even seen it coming.

Todd had smashed her in the chest with his fist. He'd escalated this all the way to a fight.

She sprawled back, choking, feeling the table tilt, and hearing a glass smash, struggling to get to her feet again.

This was bad. This was devolving all the way into an attack, and now, Todd was advancing again, with a bottle in his hand.

CHAPTER TWENTY TWO

Caitlin scrambled to her feet, but a discarded bottle on the floor caused her foot to slip, and she flailed for balance, falling again. This was turning into a seriously bad situation. She didn't like the way the other customers were crowding around or the look in Todd's eyes.

She didn't know how they were going to manage this situation, which was flaring swiftly into violence.

As she struggled, managing not to stand on the damned bottle this time, Nathan rushed back into the fray. He stood in front of Todd, just as if he was an unruly passenger on a train.

"It's okay, sir. Put the bottle down," he said calmly.

Todd looked aggressive, and he looked drunk, but he didn't hit Nathan. Instead, he settled for a verbal attack.

"It's not okay. You people are all the same. You always think you are the boss of everybody." Now, Caitlin could hear that he was not just drunk but extremely drunk.

"We just want to talk to you," Nathan said soothingly. How was he managing such a calm tone? Caitlin was impressed.

"You police are all the same. You think you can do whatever you want. You think you can just come here and take over," Todd ranted.

"It's okay," Nathan said again. "No one is taking over. We just want to ask you some questions. That's all."

Todd still looked angry, but Caitlin sensed that he was calming down a little. Somehow, Nathan's approach and demeanor was defusing his aggression. Or maybe absorbing it like a giant sponge.

"I have done nothing wrong," Todd said.

"Okay, if you have done nothing wrong, then you have nothing to worry about," Nathan said. "Let's go outside and talk like reasonable people. We can't talk in here because the music is too loud. There's no need to get angry at all."

"You don't like the music? You think you should be able to control everything? Just muscle in and tell us what to do?" Todd demanded.

"I'm just saying, let's go outside and talk," Nathan said, his tone even and soothing.

Todd looked like he was about to explode again, but he didn't. Instead, he turned and marched out of the bar, with Caitlin and Nathan right behind him. With Todd compliant, the others simmered down. There was still a hostile atmosphere, but it was no longer aggressive.

It was an interesting moment. He was an angry man, and he was drunk, but he had not attacked them again. Nathan had defused the situation, and they had a chance now to ask him some questions. Caitlin felt full of admiration for how Nathan had handled that. He'd managed to contain the situation in such a calm way and had come across as so reasonable and likable that even a drunk, aggressive man had found nothing to continue the fight. It really hit home to her that it took two to fight.

Nathan had a level of experience in defusing hostilities in a friendly way, which she hadn't gained in the FBI, when up against dangerous and violent criminals. This had given her a new insight into her partner and his skills. To think that she'd once thought he was a mere railway cop.

Of course, this man could be the dangerous criminal they were seeking, and the questioning would be the deciding factor. Caitlin reminded herself that drunk or not, he might use the opportunity of exiting the bar to escape.

As they walked through the bar, the other men were watching them, still angry and hostile. Caitlin was glad to get out of there.

And, as she watched their suspect more carefully, she became pretty sure that there would be no sudden attempt at an escape, because he was so drunk that he was literally weaving to and fro. He misjudged one of the weaves and clattered into a table, which rocked and almost fell. Nathan grasped his arm—doing so in a helpful manner rather than in an officious way.

"Let me give you a hand here," he said.

Following behind, Caitlin did note that this man was tall and strong. Broad shouldered and powerful, he would have enough physical strength to have carried the victims. That punch he'd given her had felt like a thud from a battering ram. Her breastbone was aching. He was quick to act aggressively and actually could have been arrested for that assault toward her.

But she was willing to overlook it for now if it meant he'd talk.

Outside the bar, it was quieter, and the morning air was still and cool. The street was free from cars. They moved to an outside table and chairs that was unoccupied on this cool morning with rain threatening and sat down.

Caitlin forced herself to be patient, waiting for Nathan to start the questioning. That made sense since he'd been the one to defuse the hostilities.

"Now that we can hear each other," Nathan said, "I'd like to know more about your involvement with the railways. Can you explain what happened there?"

Caitlin could see that Nathan was keen to win this man's trust and to make him believe that they just wanted to get some information. That was all.

Even so, Todd looked wary, and for a moment, Caitlin wondered if he was going to shut down right there and refuse to answer questions.

"Look, they got really hardcore about that whole thing, but the truth was there were two sides to it."

"Tell me what they were," he encouraged.

Todd glowered. "You're the police. I don't trust you. Are you going to twist this?"

"I promise, I am not going to twist it. We need information," Nathan said innocently, and Caitlin could see his strategy was to lead him on slowly but surely.

"You'd better be telling the truth," he threatened.

"I am, and I'd like to hear your truth," Nathan said.

"I was promised a sum of money, and they didn't pay me that sum of money on time. I was made to work for free! And it was hard work, too, plus, it was using my intel—illten—" He struggled with the word. "My intellectual property, in the form of the knowledge about the railways."

"How did you know about them?" Caitlin asked, hoping she could join this discussion without putting Todd off his stride.

"My dad was involved in a lot of the rebuilding and planning of the lines," he told her. "He was an engineer, and he worked on site. He kept maps and diagrams of all the railways."

"Who else would have those?" Caitlin asked. He shrugged.

"I guess everyone on the teams had access to them. That would be twenty, thirty people still living in town. But nobody took an interest. I was interested in their layout and in all those disused rails. I liked exploring, when I was a teen, seeing where they went." He hiccupped.

"And so, you ended up fighting with the railway people?"

He nodded. "They got hard assed with me, and I felt like if they can, so can I. I got hard assed right back at them. I think I might even have smacked the one guy," he remembered.

"What happened next?" Nathan asked.

"I got arrested, and they pushed it to the full extent, because they had a lot of power. I guess they wanted to make an example of me. They blamed me, because I was the one who was willing to fight back and be strong about it. They are the only people that I've ever seen who had that kind of power. I ended up with a restraining order against me. And they never paid me the damned money. I think, now, they see me as a threat.

Caitlin realized that this man was becoming paranoid once more.

"Last night," Nathan said, skillfully rerouting the conversation. "Where were you last night?"

"I was in the bar. I'm a regular, here," he said. "I help out when they need me to. Last night, the barman was busy, so I stepped in for a few hours and fetched kegs, cleaned tables, moved furniture, that kind of thing. That was all done by about five and then I stayed on, on the other side of the bar."

"Can the barman confirm that?"

"Sure, and the backroom guys, and the dishwashers. Everyone here will confirm that. You can ask any of them." He brightened. "They all know me well. They're the only people I can trust, the folks in this bar."

"Okay," Nathan said. "But before you take us to confirm this, I need something else from you."

"What's that?" he asked, suspicious again.

"I need an apology. You assaulted Agent Dare. You punched her, and you could be arrested for that. We're not arresting you right now, because you did agree to cooperate, but it doesn't mean you weren't in the wrong."

Caitlin felt stunned and surprised by this twist. So did Todd, clearly, although he looked more appalled.

"What? You want me to apologize?" he asked, astounded.

"I think it's fair," Nathan reasoned with him.

Todd shrugged. "I'll apologize if you want me to, but I want to also say that I don't know why I did it. I have been drinking, so I can't say I was in my normal state of mind."

"A short apology will do it."

To her astonishment, Todd turned to her. "Agent Dare, I do apologize. It was wrong of me to punch you like that, and I will not allow myself to behave that way again."

"Apology accepted, thank you," Caitlin said politely, reeling inwardly with surprise.

"Now, let's go take a look at that shift timetable," Nathan said. But, as they walked away, Caitlin's phone rang.

It was Aniyah, so she grabbed the call immediately.

"There's been a crisis," Aniyah said. "There's been a missing person reported from Southville. His name is Malcolm Coombes, and he didn't report for work this morning. They think he might have been abducted on the way home, because he was drinking in a bar last night, and his car's still there."

This was the worst possible news, and it felt like a hammer blow to Caitlin. The killer was demonically fast, and the bodies were piling up.

"There's something else, too," Aniyah said. "More bad news. I'm sorry, Caitlin."

She steeled herself in preparation. "What is it?" she asked.

CHAPTER TWENTY THREE

More bad news? On top of the bombshell that their suspect had an alibi, and that a new victim was missing, Aniyah had additional devastating information. Caitlin braced herself for it.

"It's the senator," Aniyah said.

"What?" Caitlin asked incredulously. This was worse than she'd feared.

"Senator Nicks, you know of him, right? He's there, in Ohio."

"Yes, I know the name."

"He called me five minutes ago."

"He called you personally?" Caitlin felt horrified at the level of interaction that Aniyah was having to deal with.

"Yes, he did. I was very surprised. He said he's just been in a meeting with the mayor and a few other officials. He's angry and wants us to find out who's responsible for the death of these victims."

They were getting scrutinized and criticized, right from the top. This sent a bolt of near panic through Caitlin.

"Tell him we're working around the clock," she said. Give or take a couple of hours of sleep, at a point where the case had stalled. But it seemed all this case was doing was stalling. Now there was another victim taken, and the body count was off the charts. Having crimes like these taking place could be a massive blow for a politician. One rogue criminal could break a career. If it became known that the small town was being terrorized, it would be a huge blow.

And that was over and above the actual toll of these crimes, and that was what lanced the deepest for her. Never mind the political implications, it was the terrible consequences for the families that got to her the most.

"I'll tell him that. Around the clock."

"We're closely following some strong leads."

"I'll tell him that too. But I'm sure all of this is what he's been told a hundred times. I mean, it won't be new to him. He won't respect this," Aniyah said, sounding worried.

"It's all we can say now." Caitlin literally felt her heart start pounding in total anguish. How frustrating was this? They were trying their best; they were literally delving into desperate waters to find this killer, and their efforts were meaningless. The powers were angry. Trying hard meant nothing and telling them so would only worsen the situation.

This was terrible, Caitlin realized, just terrible. They were now stuck in a predicament where the top-level politicians were snapping at their heels for answers. She didn't think this could get worse but feared that somehow it might.

"I'll keep in touch," Aniyah promised.

"Thank you," Caitlin said.

When she hung up, she saw Nathan approaching, without Todd, so clearly his alibi had checked out.

"What's wrong?" Nathan asked her, seeing her face.

"Senator Nicks is angry, and he's looking to make a big deal out of this. He wants answers. He's not happy."

"I'm not surprised," Nathan said, with a resigned shrug. "Why the hell should he be? I don't think I'd be happy, either. I mean, just think about it. What's going to happen next? We're going to find that new victim's body. That will make a count of four in just three days. It's a political disaster. It could sink him."

"This could sink us, too," she said, acknowledging the worst.

"Why aren't we getting further?" Nathan sounded as angry about it as she felt. "Why can't we see more?"

"Junctions in the tracks. It must mean something."

Striding out of the bar, they stood facing each other in the cold afternoon, with rain threatening. The town center was busier than it had been. People were going about their business. Down the road, Caitlin saw the church looked to have a support group or guidance session on the go in one of the side rooms. The diner was busy. School kids were walking down the sidewalk. People were going about their lives, but now with a veil of fear hanging over them—a knowledge that a killer was brutalizing this quiet area.

"What can it mean? We tried to find out! We couldn't," Nathan said.

"He knows enough to know where they live, or where they work, their habits, some of their plans," Caitlin said. "He interacts with them in some way, or at least listens in to their plans."

"Sure, it's a small town. He's in their lives. And that's why he can get to them."

"He's in their lives, or near their lives," Caitlin corrected. "He might just be an expert stalker. If he is, he's got this down to a fine art."

"How does he know about their lives?" Nathan asked, but it was something that she'd said earlier that was now sticking in her mind.

"Wait, their plans. Nathan, I've just realized something!"

"What?"

"All of them were thinking of making life changes, making moves. Moving away, going to the big city, starting a new career, that sort of thing."

"Yes, I guess they were, and it's maybe not just the move. Maybe it's more about the life changes," Nathan said thoughtfully.

"How does he know about those?"

"Maybe he's watching them, maybe he's following them," Nathan said. "He might not even know them, but he's able to get close to them in some way."

"Are they all shopping in the same place? Did they buy new travel bags somewhere?" Caitlin said.

Nathan made a face. "Now that really would be a big coincidence, everyone buying a new travel bag before the move."

"But it's a possibility."

"There's a local store. Maybe they're all buying their bags there."

"We should go there and look at the CCTV footage," Caitlin said. "Or ask them for a customer list and see if all the victims used this same store. What else would you do before you move?"

"House sales?" Nathan suggested. Now, she could see the excitement in his eyes. He was starting to buy into her theory.

"I'm not sure all of them owned their own house, but yes, that would be a good angle if they did," she said.

"Removals companies?"

"That's a great idea, I mean, all of them would have had to have packed up their homes."

They were getting lots of possibilities now. The field felt wider open again, and Caitlin felt elated that they had come up with new theories.

Now, all they needed to do was to make a list, decide which one was the most promising, and chase it down. Before too long, she was sure that they would be moving forward again.

"I think we start with the removals companies," Nathan said.

Caitlin was about to disagree with him and say that she thought the CCTV footage in the travel store was a better angle when her phone rang.

It was Aniyah again, and she felt slightly sick as she answered. "Hey, Aniyah," she said, waiting for the hammer blow that she was sure would follow.

Aniyah's voice was focused and intent.

"Caitlin, they've found that abducted victim on the tracks, near a junction heading out of Clearwell, on the way to Mayfield."

Caitlin felt defeat fill her. A fourth victim. Another kill. Would this horror ever end?

But then, she realized Aniyah was continuing, and that her whole tone of voice, the way she was speaking, sounded different. Excited.

"You need to get there as soon as possible, and I'm going to send you the coordinates right away. Because this victim is still alive! He wasn't killed. He's still alive, Caitlin, and this changes everything!"

CHAPTER TWENTY FOUR

Alive! This victim was alive? Renewed purpose flared within Caitlin as she and Nathan sprinted for the car.

By the time they reached it, the coordinates had come through. This was on a section of railway track that looked to be about four miles from where they were.

"How did this happen?" she asked Nathan as they sped away from the bar. “Why is he alive? I’m glad, but I’m also very confused.”

"He could be badly injured," Nathan warned. "We don’t know yet what condition he’s in, and he might not be in a position to tell us much."

Caitlin knew she had to manage her expectations. She mustn't be too hopeful. But she couldn't help thinking that this represented a major breakthrough in the case.

"Did he do this intentionally? Or is he getting careless?"

"I don't know, but we can’t assume he's going to give up any time soon. It's not like he's lost interest. He's not going to stop." Nathan's voice held the same anger that Caitlin had felt earlier.

"I know. I know," Caitlin said. "But I can't help thinking this is a major development. If we can find out why he's done this, maybe it will lead us to what he's planning next."

"This could be deliberate," Nathan said. “He could be leading us away from what he’s planning next.”

Caitlin nodded. "This is a small-town area. By now, he knows that we're onto him. He's got to know we're trying to catch him. Maybe he's just set this one up as some sort of decoy."

Gripping the wheel, she sped on. This was something they needed to remember. No way was he planning to stop.

They were out in the countryside now, driving into a landscape that was smothered in clouds heavy with rain. Once again, Caitlin felt that she had to keep her hopes in check and not get too excited, but she could feel her heart racing.

Ahead, she saw a police car and an ambulance parked on the side of the road. Beyond that, a muddy trail led out into the fields. Caitlin got out of the car and jogged along the trail. This time, it wasn't as far of a distance to the railway lines. Only a couple hundred yards, and the scene came into view.

Two police officers were standing beside the tracks, together with a young man in a knit cap who was talking to them excitedly, and behind them, two paramedics were at work.

Caitlin rushed up. She saw the paramedics were working on a man dressed in a woolen jacket and jeans. His hands must have been tied behind him, Caitlin saw, because a length of discarded nylon rope lay nearby, as did a pile of tarps.

The medics were wrapping the man carefully in a blanket before assisting him onto a stretcher. He looked to be conscious, she thought hopefully.

"Morning," she said to the small group of people. "Railway task force unit here. We're very relieved that this man is alive. What's the situation here, please?"

The policeman stepped forward. "We were called by this witness," he indicated the young man in the cap. The police didn't have to say more. Clearly thrilled to be able to tell his story again, the man turned to Caitlin and Nathan.

"I was on a trail run about an hour ago, and I heard shouting coming from somewhere. It sounded like someone was calling for help. I followed the noise, and I saw the gentleman. He was lying there," the man said, pointing to the figure on the stretcher. "He was shivering and tied up and in a very bad way. I took a look, and I saw the rope around his hands and feet, and I immediately remembered that story I heard on the news yesterday. I called 911 immediately and stayed with him until they got there. I got the ropes around his wrists and ankles undone and gave him my jacket and some water. He was freezing cold obviously. I hope he'll be okay."

"Thank you so much for helping him," Caitlin said, grateful for these potentially lifesaving actions.

She moved over to the victim, who was sipping what looked like tea from a steaming flask the paramedics were offering.

One of them looked up at her, cheerfully. "The patient, Malcolm Coombes, looks to be in okay shape," he said. "He has a slight concussion and looks to be suffering from mild exposure after a full night and most of a morning in the cold, but there's nothing seriously wrong that we can tell. We're going to transport him to the hospital to get fully checked out, though."

"Can I speak to him?" Caitlin asked.

"Sure," the paramedic said. "We need to get him into the ambulance as fast as we can, into the warmth, so why don't you speak to him on the way?" He turned back to his patient. "Sir, are you sure you're good to walk?"

"Yes, I can walk," Malcolm said in a hoarse voice. The paramedics helped him carefully to his feet, and one of them slung his arm over their shoulder while the other packed up the stretcher.

Caitlin saw that this man was in his thirties, with dark hair, and a shadow of stubble on his face. His hair looked matted, and she guessed he'd also had a blow to the head.

"Can you tell me what happened, Malcolm?" she asked, hoping he'd be able to remember enough.

He paused, frowning, picking his way forward as if this was all too much for him to handle.

"I was out drinking at the local bar last night. I don't remember anything for a while after leaving, so I guess I was attacked, hit on the head." He raised a hand gingerly to his matted hair and flinched.

Caitlin paced along beside him as he made his slow progress down the track.

"When I woke, I was somewhere else. It was totally dark. I was lying against a steel wall of some kind," he said. "Then a light shone in my eyes, and this guy started interrogating me, asking me about my plans."

"And what did you tell him?" Nathan asked.

"I didn't understand at first. I mean, I was totally confused and scared. But eventually I realized he must be referring to my move—I'm moving across the state to start a new job, in a new branch of the company I work for."

"Did you tell him you were moving?"

"You know, it was so weird—the whole setup, the way he was asking—I thought to myself that it might be better if I lied and said I wasn't moving. Reason being, I knew the insurance lady, Edna, slightly, and I know she was killed. I thought maybe he's going to kill me if I said I was going. So, I made up an excuse why I'd thought about it and decided not to go."

Caitlin's eyes widened. Quick thinking and a lucky guess had saved this man's life.

"Then he put this cloth over my face. I guess it was chloroform, or something nasty, because everything went gray, and I was out of it for a while more, and then when I woke up again, I was on these tracks. It was early morning, and I was freezing cold. I struggled and shouted and luckily someone heard."

They had now reached the ambulance. The paramedics helped the man up into the back. One of them rushed around to the front and started it up, getting the heater cranked high.

"Who knew you were moving?"

"Well, everyone at my work. I work for a landscaping and yard maintenance company. So, they all knew. And a few people from the local church knew, as our company maintains their grounds for free."

"Anyone you spoke to or consulted with?"

The man frowned. "Actually, there was someone that I was planning to go and see, but I never did."

"And who was that?"

"He was recommended to me by someone at work. His name is Des Jenkins. He works in town, and he's like a psychologist, a life coach, that sort of thing. I thought it would be good to book a consult with him. To check I was making the right move."

"And did you go and see him?"

"No, I didn't. We emailed back and forth, and I told him about the opportunity, but I hadn't gotten around to actually going and seeing him, and then I decided to take the plunge and go for the new job regardless."

"But he knew you were considering it?" Caitlin's focus felt sharp. This was a potential breakthrough.

"Yes, he did."

Looking grateful, Malcolm lay down on the bed, and the paramedic quickly covered him with an insulation blanket.

"Thank you so much, and I hope you recover soon. We'll be in touch if we need to," Caitlin said.

Finally, they had identified a person who counseled and advised people who were thinking of making a big life decision. Des Jenkins was presumably a trusted member of the community.

Had he misused that trust?

The first step was to find out if he had interacted with any other of the victims, and as they headed back to the car, Nathan was already on the phone.

"Mr. Lawson?" he said, and Caitlin realized he'd called Edna's husband as a first choice. "I wonder if you could tell me something urgently, please?"

He waited for the husband's reply and then continued.

"Did your wife seek counseling, or advice, from anyone on her divorce or her move?"

He waited. Then nodded. "Thank you," he said.

He turned to Caitlin. "Edna took advice from the local church ladies' group, and from Des Jenkins. She had two sessions with him. Apparently, she wasn't happy and said he was much too intrusive and was trying to micromanage her life for her."

Now, Caitlin's eyebrows just about hit her hairline.

Des Jenkins was a prime suspect, and there was no time to waste in getting face to face with him.

Talking someone out of a decision hadn't worked. Had he then taken drastic action?

CHAPTER TWENTY FIVE

Laverne Mills couldn't believe it. Today was the day she was going to taste freedom. At last.

It might be a cold, gray, fall day, but for her, it represented a turning point in her life. For five years now, she'd been with the abusive, angry, manipulative man that she had now realized was a narcissist.

When she'd first moved in with him, she'd thought he was dreamy, and she'd been lucky to meet him. Now, she felt like a fool. A wounded, broken fool who'd endured far too much emotional and physical abuse.

She remembered how she'd been when she met him, a confident twenty-three-year-old who believed the world was at her feet. And then gradually, he'd started controlling her life, eroding her self-image, and estranging her from her support system.

She had convinced herself that he would change, that he would stop abusing her, that it was her fault, and if she could only behave better, then she'd be treated better. Classic tactics, she now realized.

"I'm leaving you for good now," she said aloud. She could, because for once, it was safe to do that.

Her husband was halfway through a ten-day business trip for work. He hadn't wanted to go. Not at all. He'd been very angry to have had to fly out of state for such a long time to attend a business conference and expo followed by a five-day management training session, but he hadn't had a choice, and spouses were not allowed to go along. He'd tried that, of course, not wanting her to be out of his clutches for a minute.

The day after he'd left, she'd broken. She had booked herself in for a counseling session and she'd received some excellent, calm advice from a trusted source.

And now, three days later, she was ready to leave, and she had her support structure in place. She was going to fly out of state, too, but not to New York, where he was. Nowhere near there, in fact. She was going all the way to Florida, where an old school friend would put her up for a while until she got herself on her feet and found a new job.

He might come looking for her.

"I need to be prepared for that," she said. "I need to get a house share, some sort of accommodation where my name isn't recorded. I need to stay under the radar for a while. But Florida's a far way to go, anyway."

At least she was now committed to her decision. She was going to get free of him and start a new life.

She stared at herself in the mirror as she passed it, smoothing back her brown hair, which he complained about constantly. It was too frizzy, too unruly, too ugly. But at the same time, he wouldn't let her change it or cut it or color it, because then other men might look at her. What a situation to be stuck in.

She didn't think she was as ugly or incapable as she'd come to believe. She knew she'd used to think of herself as attractive, with her slim build, her wide, blue eyes, and her girl next door charm.

Maybe she could rebuild herself, get back to that mindset, that happy confidence that had used to characterize her thoughts and her actions.

She would treat this as a new start, a new day, and remember that she was on the cusp of a new life. And she needn't be scared for long. Soon, she would celebrate! It had taken time, but she'd managed to squirrel some money away from the job she had in the back office of a car rental department. She'd always thought that one day, if the opportunity came along, she could use it. It was enough for the air ticket and to reimburse her friend for the accommodation and a little more besides.

She would go out and buy herself a new outfit. She would do her hair, get a chestnut or mahogany color, and update her makeup—he never allowed her to wear any.

She would try to find an old picture of herself, when she was happy, and put it by her bedside. She'd work on her confidence every day.

That was the other thing she'd learned during her counseling session. She was going to need to work on her self-esteem, to rebuild her self-image to be more positive.

And, most exciting of all, she'd find a new job working with people. She was a speech coach; she loved to help people with public speaking, voice control, and presenting a better image. He had forbidden that. It would involve talking to other men, which was not allowed.

The few interactions she'd had with men, the few conversations, always made her feel guilty, and she remembered them word for word.

But that was behind her now, and it all lay ahead of her, within grasping distance. She gazed out at the gray, chilly dawn and shivered slightly. She was going to be free. Finally free.

Laverne checked the time. She had less than three hours before her flight took off. She had to get a move on. First things first, she must get her last few possessions from the shed and then she needed to call a cab to get herself to the airport.

She still felt a flash of fear when she thought about him arriving back unexpectedly. That was making her extremely nervous. He would be furious if he saw her planning to leave.

Or, worse, he would pretend to be fine with it, and the day after she had gone, he would be waiting for her, wherever she had gone to.

But at least, for now, he was safely in New York, and she'd checked the schedule. For the next three days, he was booked up with presentations. He was on the company's program. There was no way he could leave, or at least, so she reassured herself.

Now, she just needed to go out to the shed and get her sun hat and sunglasses which had been stored away in there.

She walked out of the house, closing the front door because the wind was whistling in.

Then Laverne headed for the shed, but as she did so, the bushes outside her house seemed to erupt, and something—someone—emerged. Her first, terrified, illogical thought was that this was her husband, that he'd found her despite all her efforts to stay hidden, and that this was it, the end—that it was all over.

And then, she knew nothing more as a hard thump on her head caused the world to go gray and blurry and then flicker out completely.

*

When she awoke—muzzy headed, terrified, and with a splitting headache—she found herself in a darkened room. She had no idea where she was. Or how much time had passed. She thought a few hours might have passed, and she wondered if she'd been drugged in some way, because there was a terrible, chemical smell in her nose, and her mouth felt very dry, with a bitter, unpleasant taste.

Panic flared inside her. What had happened? Frantically, she tried to remember what had played out, what disastrous turn her life had taken. Her last memory was of walking toward the shed.

And then nothing. And now this.

She tried to move, but she was tied down. Her arms and legs were bound, and she was lying in what seemed to be a dark, metal cave. Who had drugged her? Was this his doing?

No, she didn't think so. She didn't think he'd known. There was no way he could have known. He was away at a company conference!

Who, then?

She felt numb and shocked, and her brain was not functioning at its usual level. It was hard to think, hard to remember.

Then, she flinched, recoiling as a light pierced her eyes, searing through them. The next moment, a deep, hoarse, gravelly voice spoke from a yard or two away, "So, Laverne? What's your next move? Tell me, what have you decided? Are you going to go?"

She knew the voice! She caught her breath as she realized who the speaker was. After all, she was a trained speech therapist. She could match voices to people easily, and she hadn't met many people since her disastrous marriage.

She knew the speaker and had interacted with him recently. For sure, he wasn't who she'd thought. He was a psychopath, and she'd never known it. What she didn't know, was what her answer should be, because the railway murders that she'd heard about meant the wrong answer would surely be fatal.

Taking all her courage, she made the decision.

In a shaky voice, she began to reply.

CHAPTER TWENTY SIX

As they drove into town, heading for the offices where Des Jenkins worked, Nathan took the case forward with yet more background research on this new, strong suspect.

His next call was to Audrey's brother. "Morning. I'm calling from the railway task force. We have a question," he asked. "Would you know if Audrey spoke to anyone regarding her decision to move? Did she take advice or counseling?"

He listened to the reply, thanked him, and cut the call.

"He said yes, she took advice from a few different sources, and she mentioned that she'd had some kind of a discussion with someone in town who offered support, but he doesn't know who or where."

Even so, it added to the weight of evidence. That, Caitlin could see. Des Jenkins was in town and was so well placed to hear about changes. It was, after all, what he did.

Des Jenkins had his offices in a small commercial park on the town's main road, nothing more than half a block of well-equipped buildings that looked more like cottages than offices.

There were several cars parked outside the buildings, including three directly outside the place that was signposted as *"Desmond Jenkins—Psychologist & Life Coach."*

Caitlin walked up the three stairs that led to the entrance, wondering what would play out when she and Nathan headed inside. That would depend on whether he was guilty or not, she knew.

In the lobby, an attractive, blonde receptionist was on duty at the desk. She looked to be in her early twenties and was twirling locks of honey-colored hair around her fingers while scrolling idly through her phone.

"Morning," Caitlin said briskly.

The blonde looked up, surprise changing to annoyance as she saw them there.

"How can I help?" she asked in rather unhelpful tones.

"We are from the railway task force, and we're here regarding the recent crimes in the area. We need to speak to Mr. Jenkins," Caitlin said.

"I'm sorry, but he's busy with a client," she said automatically, glancing at the computer screen.

"I'm afraid this is urgent, and we'll need to speak to him now," Caitlin said.

The receptionist made a show of looking at her watch. "He's got back-to-back consults all morning. He's just starting a new one now."

"Then you'll want to interrupt the consult before he gets going with it and tell him we're here," Caitlin said, getting tired of her unhelpful attitude. "Just go in and knock on his door. Explain that we are police, and this is a murder case, and it's urgent. If you don't, then I will."

The blonde looked doubtful, but clearly, Caitlin's intentions were convincing enough because she got up, smoothed down her skirt, and headed to the door.

Moments later, the door opened, and Des Jenkins himself stood there.

He was a good-looking man—tall, tanned, and with a full head of sandy-blond hair. He looked to be in his early forties and was dressed in a crisp, white shirt and dark suit pants. He had a gentle smile on his face.

"I understand you're from the police?"

"Correct, sir," Caitlin said. "We need a quick word." How quick would depend, of course, on what he said—or didn't say.

"Could you please come into the consulting room?" he said. "I am expecting a patient to arrive any minute."

So, nobody was here yet? Caitlin turned and gave the receptionist a meaningful glare. She didn't like being lied to. The receptionist looked away, pouting.

Jenkins stepped aside, and Caitlin marched in, already feeling irritated with the unhelpful attitude here and wondering if it pointed to a cover up. She'd been momentarily mad at the receptionist, yes, but staff did what their bosses told them to.

Nathan came in behind her, and she found herself in an office that was well organized, with a huge, wooden desk at the far end of the room. There was an array of comfortable-looking chairs, and a bookshelf and coffee table displaying a range of books on psychology, therapy, goal setting and mind power.

Caitlin guessed that the life coach was one of those people who presented himself as having a solution to every problem.

"Please, take a seat."

The three of them sat down, with Caitlin taking the chair next to the desk, and Jenkins moving to the swivel chair behind it. On the desk, Caitlin noticed a framed photo of an attractive, dark-haired woman who was presumably Mrs. Jenkins. And on the walls, she saw framed photos of old steam trains. Her gaze lingered on those for a while, wondering if this was significant.

He waited for them to sit, then he sat himself and leaned forward with his hands clasped and a smile on his face.

"I'm afraid I can't answer any questions regarding my clients," he said. "I'm very sorry. Patient confidentiality, you understand?"

"We're here because at least one of your patients has been murdered. One narrowly escaped death. And we need to know more about what you discussed with them, and your attitude toward the decisions you were counseling them on."

He looked startled.

"I don't know about any murders," he said.

"You don't?" Caitlin asked. How was that possible when the murders were the talk of the town?

"I seldom watch the news. I find it fills one's brain with negativity," he explained.

"You were approached by Malcolm Coombes recently about a move he was planning."

He frowned. "I don't recall actually booking a session with him," he said.

"Even so, you got many of the details on his circumstances. That was recently. And now, let's talk about a week or two earlier. You also counseled Edna Lawson," Caitlin pushed. "That was a booked session, if I am correct?"

Now, he looked alarmed. "Mrs. Lawson? Er, yes. Yes, I did counsel her."

"I understand she was unhappy with your advice," Caitlin said. Now, Jenkins was looking seriously alarmed.

"What did she tell you?" he asked. "Because I don't want to breach any confidentiality here."

“She apparently told her husband that she wasn't happy with the sessions, that she felt you were overly intrusive, and that you were trying to micromanage her," Caitlin said.

Des Jenkins looked surprised. "That's not true," he said. "I was trying to help her make a more informed decision, and I think she was feeling pressure from her friends and her husband. I was trying to get her to understand that her decision was hers, and that she needed to be comfortable with it."

"You didn't end up making the decision for her?" Caitlin asked.

"I—er, no. I wouldn't do that," he said, fidgeting.

"Because, based on the evidence, someone who knows a lot about these victims' lives has been killing them if he feels they are taking the wrong path in life."

"It was not me!" Defensiveness and anger now emanated from the tall psychologist. "I find these questions of yours to be frivolous and in fact, insulting. I must ask you to leave!"

"Not so fast, please, sir," Nathan said calmly. "Where were you last night? And the previous night, from early evening onward? We need to confirm your alibi."

"I am not willing to do that. I was conducting sessions with patients! I have no need of any alibi being confirmed," he blustered, now looking thoroughly put out and slightly guilty.

"I'm afraid it's either that, or we need to consider you as a suspect," Caitlin said. "Otherwise, we're going to have to take you in, and you'll be interrogated more formally. You can ask for a lawyer to be present, of course."

Jenkins paled, and he looked so nervous now that he was practically shaking. "I wasn't anywhere near these victims," he said.

"Were you here, in your rooms? If you were seeing patients, I presume so?" Caitlin said. "In that case, your receptionist can confirm the bookings?"

"No, no. I don't want to bring her into it!"

"Why not?"

"I—she knows nothing about the after-hours consults," he explained. "Those are organized by me."

That sounded extremely irregular to Caitlin. They were definitely venturing into that territory now.

"Then please, sir, confirm you were here," Nathan said. "We need proof."

Des Jenkins took a deep breath and nodded. "I was here," he said, avoiding their eyes. "And there's nothing more to be said."

"Mr. Jenkins, you haven't given us a shred of proof. We can't just take your word, especially when you are refusing to disclose important facts. You're going to have to choose one way or the other. Either you can be questioned in the police station, in the presence of a lawyer if you prefer, or you can volunteer information to us now."

He looked frantic now, and his eyes darted to the door. If he was considering making a run for it, Caitlin was not going to give him the chance. There was something seriously untoward going on; that, she was sure of.

The next moment, Jenkins snapped completely. "I was here!" he roared, with a look of rage in his eyes. The sound reverberated around the room. He leaped to his feet, stormed around the desk, and grabbed Caitlin by the front of her shirt. In one swift movement, he moved his face close to hers, so close she could smell his breath—minty, with an undertone of cigarette smoke. "Stop harassing me, you interfering bitch!" he shouted.

Feeling furious, she shoved him back, wrenching his fingers off her blouse. This questioning was triggering Jenkins. Triggering him big time. Now, he was a completely different person from the controlled, charming façade he'd presented when they walked in.

The next moment, Nathan had jumped to his feet too. He grabbed the psychologist's arm and yanked him away.

"You're coming in, now. Assaulting an officer of the law is grounds for arrest," he said firmly. "You're guilty of that. And you're going to stay in custody until we find out what else you've done."

CHAPTER TWENTY SEVEN

Pulling up outside the local police station, Caitlin felt relieved to be getting out of the car. Her eardrums were ringing. Handcuffed for the trip, Jenkins had been shouting, cursing, threatening, and pleading in turns.

Without a doubt, this man was guilty. Now, they needed to find out: what was he guilty of? Was he their killer?

She hoped that he would crack, and confess, and that the case would be over. Otherwise, there would be more deaths, more tragedies, and she had no doubt that the powers up high would be furious. Caitlin wasn't usually a fearful person, but the thought of the political wheels turning behind the scenes was terrifying to her.

If this was their suspect, and they could close the case, it would be the best outcome.

She knew, though, that everything rode on this questioning and on what they could get Jenkins to say.

The police station was starting to feel familiar to her. They'd already dragged one reluctant suspect in while on this case. Now, for a second one.

"Can we use your interview room again, please?" Caitlin asked, going in ahead of Nathan, who was escorting Jenkins, in his handcuffs, inside.

"Sure," the officer on duty said. "I hope this crime is solved soon," he added. "I've been fielding a lot of concerned calls from members of the public, and one or two from the local press. We have a hotline in place for information, but so far, nothing useful has come in."

"I hope it does," Caitlin agreed. Any information might help them now.

The phone began ringing again, and Caitlin hurried through to prepare the interview room while Nathan completed the processing of the suspect.

She got the chairs in order, checked that the recording device was working, and then Nathan appeared at the door with the psychologist in tow.

They sat Jenkins down on the opposite side of the desk.

"We're going to resume our questioning from earlier," Caitlin said, taking a seat herself. "We were running into problems when you refused to tell us what you were doing last night, and also the night before last. Are you ready to tell us that?"

"I will not have you violating my privacy this way," Jenkins complained, his voice full of anger. "I have the right to privacy. I have the right for you not to go digging around in my personal business."

"The victims also have rights. And according to you, this wasn't personal business but seeing patients," Caitlin pointed out. "Were you at your premises last night? And the night before? If you have been seeing patients after normal hours, why is there no record of their visits, and why doesn't your receptionist know about these visits?" Nathan pressed him.

"Patient confidentiality prevents me from disclosing that," he snarled at them.

"Were these patients life coaching or psychology patients? Why are you not able to disclose any details?"

Did the patients even exist? Caitlin was now wondering. It seemed like this psychologist was doing everything he could to evade their questions. Was "seeing patients" the excuse he gave his wife for going out at night to conduct these torturous interrogations on his victims before dumping their bodies on the tracks?

Of course, there were other reasons he could have given his wife as an excuse to be away from home, and Caitlin knew only too well that a good-looking man who was dealing with patients in crisis and at a crossroads might have been tempted to get a little too close to some of them. That was a definite possibility. Highly unethical and one for which he could lose his license to practice. And that could also be why he was so stubbornly refusing to talk.

"And what about the night before that? Were you here on the premises then?"

"I will not answer any more questions about my patients," Jenkins said firmly. "My records are confidential, and your questioning is biased and intrusive."

"You need to answer these questions, Dr. Jenkins," she insisted, her voice firm but level. "Were you at your premises?"

"I was at the premises," he said, but he looked shifty as he spoke. Caitlin didn't believe him.

"Who were these patients? How did they make payment to you?"

"I have the right not to disclose any information, and I will exercise that right."

"What did you tell your wife? Does your wife know about these nighttime consultations with patients? Why doesn't your receptionist know?"

Now, anger was flaring in their suspect again. "You are being insulting! These questions are completely out of line. I've changed my mind! Get me my lawyer, now. I'm not saying any more until I speak to my lawyer."

Caitlin couldn't feel more frustrated by this man's stubbornness. He was being totally evasive and stonewalling them at every opportunity. Now, he was demanding a lawyer. That would delay this further.

While Nathan organized for him to call his lawyer, Caitlin stepped outside, needing to cool off, calm down, and figure out how to deal with this stubborn man, who was clearly hiding something.

She paced up and down the corridor, feeling her stress levels spiking. She could have grabbed Jenkins by his broad shoulders and shaken him! That was how mad at him she felt. He was obstructing the course of justice, and they were no closer to any answers.

Nathan walked out, closing the door, looking equally stressed.

"There was something interesting I noticed when he called his lawyer," he said.

"What was that?" Caitlin asked.

He spoke to him briefly, and it seemed he was purposefully mumbling, but I picked up the word "again." I think he's been in trouble before and has needed his lawyer to pull him out of it."

Again? That was a good question. What had happened the last time?

"If he has any kind of record, even something like dropped charges, or a visit from the police, we need to know what it is," Caitlin said.

"Do you think the officer at the front desk would know?" Nathan asked.

"I'm sure they could pull the information for us. After all, Jenkins is a local here, and if there were any complaints or problems, they would have come to this police station."

"It's going to be important for us to know that." Caitlin knew it could make all the difference.

They hurried back to the front desk, leaving their suspect to stew, and Caitlin hoped, rethink his uncooperative mindset.

At the front desk, the officer was busy on yet another a call. "I see, ma'am. I understand. We'll definitely look into it." He scribbled down some notes quickly. "Thank you for calling," he said.

He looked up, his face serious. "I'm glad you came through. I was about to go and call you."

"Has more information come in?" Caitlin asked.

"It has, and I'm not sure if this is our killer, or something different."

"What is it?" Anxiety now clenched at Caitlin's stomach. "What's happened?"

"A friend of a local woman called Laverne Mills has just called. Laverne was apparently about to get out of an abusive relationship. The friend was expecting her to call when she was on board the airplane. She didn't call, and the friend now can't get hold of her. She's asked us if we can check up on her." He looked at them, doubt and fear in his eyes.

Caitlin felt the same way. And so did Nathan, as she glanced at him.

"About to get out of an abusive relationship? That's a decision, it's a junction, it's exactly why the killer would target her," Caitlin said.

"She could just be hiding away, or have gone to a shelter, or even made it up with the husband again, though," Nathan pointed out. "You know how often abused women end up rethinking their bad decisions. Or he could have come home, and trouble could have followed."

A surprise arrival of the husband could be the reason, but even so, Caitlin was convinced that someone, somehow, had known about it.

"You stay here and look through the archives to see if Jenkins has any kind of a record," she said. "I'm going to go and see what's happening at Laverne's house, and if there are any signs she was taken. Please, give me her friend's phone number," she asked the officer. "If Laverne consulted someone before making this big life decision, it's possible the friend knows who it is."

CHAPTER TWENTY EIGHT

Caitlin jumped into the car and sped out of the police station, swinging onto the road, and hitting the gas as she headed to Laverne's home address.

As she drove, she kept trying to call Amy, Laverne's friend in Florida, but Amy wasn't picking up. Caitlin tried to reassure herself that Amy was most likely panicking, too, trying to get hold of her friend and calling the airport to see if she'd maybe taken a later flight. That was what Caitlin would do in the circumstances.

For now, though, the most she could do was leave a message, because she was arriving at Laverne's house, a corner home at the end of a quiet road. It was a neat, well-kept place, with an immaculately mowed yard. It looked like a happy, comfortable home, and it gave Caitlin shivers to think that it had been a place where an abusive husband had driven his wife to the point of leaving.

She pulled up outside and approached the home cautiously, because she had no idea what was playing out here. If the husband had come home, there could be a full-scale fight in progress. The wife could be locked away somewhere, and the husband might answer the door casually, full of charm, pretending nothing was wrong.

But when she walked up to the front door, Caitlin saw that it was actually open a crack. She tapped on it loudly.

"Hello?" she called. "Anyone there?"

Seeing it was open anyway, there was surely no harm in pushing it just a little wider? Caitlin couldn't see a problem with doing that. Her "get things done" reputation was coming to the fore here she knew, because this was not strictly speaking within her mandate, but the wind could have blown it open after all.

She swung the door wide and peeked inside.

Then she caught her breath. A neatly packed travel bag and a purse stood in front of the hall table. Laverne had been ready to go. On her way out. There was no sign of a fight in the house, and no sight or sound of anyone inside. Just to be sure, Caitlin called again, loudly, but the house felt empty.

And then, she jumped as her phone rang. This was Amy, calling back, and just in time. Caitlin grabbed up the call.

"Agent Dare?" Amy sounded anxious. "I listened to your message."

"I'm at Laverne's home. There are travel bags in the hall, and she's not here," Caitlin said, getting the information across as quick and calmly as she could.

Amy caught her breath in a shuddering sob. "What could have happened? Do you think he came back, or is it that … that serial killer you mentioned in your message?"

"We have to assume she has been taken," Caitlin said.

“No! I don’t believe it,” the friend said, sounding hysterical with worry. But there was no time for that. In a loud, strong, steady voice, Caitlin pushed forward to get what she needed.

"Please, stay calm. You might have information that can help us find her. Were you in close contact with her before she left, ma’am?"

A few gasps told her that Amy was pulling herself together.

"Y … yes. Especially in the last few days when her husband was on the business trip. We were making nonstop plans," Amy said.

"Did she mention if she went for counseling, took any advice from anyone?" Caitlin said, holding her breath that there would be an answer.

"She went to a support group at the local church down the road," Amy said. "I believe it was very helpful. She said that they have helped a lot of people grappling with big life decisions."

The church! That big, central church, one of the most imposing and busy institutions in town. Now that Caitlin was thinking about it, other people had also mentioned that church. Edna Lawson had attended a support group at the church as well as consulting with Jenkins.

The church was the common thread, she now felt sure of it.

"Who was in charge there? Who ran the meetings?"

"The minister herself, a lovely woman in her sixties. Minister Benn, her name was, I think."

That ruled her out. A lovely woman in her sixties was not their suspect. He was a strong man. But Caitlin knew that a strong man must have somehow overheard what had happened in those meetings. They were getting closer.

"Did Laverne say anything else about them?"

"No, that's all. Will she be okay, do you know?" Amy sounded anxious.

That depended on the answer she gave the killer, Caitlin knew, with a clench of her heart. What would an abused woman, leaving her husband, say in those circumstances? Would it be a yes? She feared so.

"We're going to do all we can," she said as a compromise. "Thank you so much for your help." Ending the call, Caitlin got back in the car and raced to the church, hoping to follow the trail to its conclusion.

This centrally located building—so peaceful looking with its pale, brick walls and its beautifully groomed gardens, with trimmed grass and flower beds full of roses and lavender—was where a killer had been at work.

Now, at last, she was going to find out who it was. She parked outside and rushed into the church, turning in the direction of the church offices, hoping someone would be there who knew what happened in these support groups and who could have overheard.

There was the office ahead, with an "All Welcome" sign on the door, and the sound of tapping on a keyboard coming from inside. Knocking briefly, Caitlin pushed the door open at the same time that the elderly assistant inside said, "Come in?"

She stepped inside, into the peaceful, little office, with framed Bible verses and laminated church circulars on the walls, and a small vase of flowers on the reception desk.

"Good morning," the assistant smiled. "How can I help?"

"I'm from the police, and it's in connection with the murders," she explained.

"Oh dear," the woman said. Her eyes widened. "We are all so worried about that, but I'm not sure how the church can help? Is there something related to these crimes that's linked to us in any way?"

"There may be," Caitlin said. "I wanted to know if you could tell me about the support group that goes on here?"

"Support group?" the assistant looked up, her face lighting up with sudden interest. "Oh, yes, we have that. What a blessing it is to those in need."

"How does it work?" Caitlin was impatient to get to the point, but she needed to get this woman onside.

"The minister conducts them, either in a group, or else individually, whichever people prefer. They are very helpful and in fact one of the most popular activities. We welcome anyone to them, whether they are a part of our church or not."

"Who else is involved? Who helps organize them?"

Now, finally, she got her lead. "Tony does that. He's not here today, though." The woman glanced at the empty desk to her right.

"And who is Tony?" Caitlin asked, keeping her voice casual. She didn't want this helpful woman to clam up on her in an effort to protect her colleague.

"Tony Lang. He assists with the support group, organizes the catering for the sessions, and also does some handyman work around the church. He's been with us for about six months. He's a lovely man, so helpful and friendly. Amazing after what he's been through."

"And what has he been through?"

Now, she could see that the woman was starting to get suspicious of all these questions. She answered more hesitantly this time.

"Well, it was very sad. I suppose I can tell you. It is a personal tragedy."

"I could look it up or ask someone else, but if you're willing to tell me, it would help us get a quicker picture," Caitlin said, with a calm smile that took every ounce of effort she had.

"Well, he used to work in a corporate environment, and he was going to be promoted and transferred. But his family was involved in a terrible accident en route."

"What happened?"

"A railway crossing wasn't working correctly, and the car stalled, and between one thing and another, his entire family was killed by a train. Everyone in the car died. He said he blamed himself for ages, for making the wrong decision. Tragic, really." The assistant looked at Caitlin sadly.

Tragic as it might be, but now, at last, Caitlin had her killer.

She knew who had been committing these crimes and why. Everything added up. This man, this Tony Lang, had suffered a psychotic break after his family had been killed. And working for the church, seeing other people embark on life decisions like his own, he'd started killing them rather than allowing them to make the move. Seeing his own family had been annihilated, that was the twisted logic that was now driving his murderous actions.

Where was Tony?

He had a victim and an agenda. Now, Caitlin urgently needed to find out his location.

CHAPTER TWENTY NINE

A killer with a scarred, tortured mind. A clear psychotic break and a strong motive to kill. Caitlin had every puzzle piece in place except for the most important one of all.

Where was he now with his latest victim?

If she could find that out, she might have the chance to save her. But how was he choosing his sites? There were hundreds of junctions. They were so numerous and complex they'd even defeated the expert that had been brought in to map them. As she hurried back to the car, she was agonizing over the possibilities.

Where could the next killing site be?

The junctions were a metaphor for him, that was clear. They were very meaningful to him for very obvious reasons.

But his family had been killed at a railroad crossing, Caitlin then realized, frowning. Were those also mapped? And given the circumstances, was he maybe seeking out junctions that were close to railroad crossings?

Now that Caitlin was thinking along those lines, the maps she'd looked at were resurfacing in her memory. She thought she might just be onto something here.

She found the maps in the car and spread them out over the hood of the vehicle. The maps showed the main railroad lines. They didn't show all the junctions because some of those were on old sections of track.

But they did show all the railroad crossings, and Caitlin hissed in a breath as she realized that there weren't too many of those. There were seven in total that she could find in the wider area.

"Were all the previous bodies dumped near railroad crossings?" she muttered to herself, staring at the maps, marking off the sites, grabbing the page as a gust of wind threatened to sweep it off the car's hood.

She checked the map carefully and then double checked herself again, feeling excitement now boiling inside her. It was true. All the bodies had been found within half a mile of a railroad crossing. So, if her reasoning was correct, he was looking for the railroad crossing first, and then, he was choosing the closest junction point where old met new.

Now that was the break they needed.

"Seven crossings in total." Carefully, she mapped them out, tracing the route to the nearest visible junction.

There were two crossings remaining in the area, and surely one of those was where he was now.

The closest one was nearby, she saw. In fact, it was only a mile away, just out of town. And the junction that was nearest to it was only a few hundred yards away from that. She could get there in a couple of minutes.

This was a hunch. It was a strong hunch, but there was no hard evidence supporting it. And Nathan was busy interrogating a witness with a criminal record.

She called him all the same, but his phone went to voicemail. She guessed that he must be back in that interrogation room, hoping to get the truth out of a very guilty man.

Caitlin decided that this time, it would be best to go alone. She got into her car and headed out to the tracks, feeling nervous and resolute and as if everything hinged on what would happen next.

The drive took literally a couple of minutes, and during that time, Caitlin played the facts of the case in her head, again and again. It all added up. It all linked. It all made sense. Now, it all rested on finding him there. And if he wasn't here, she had only one chance left.

This junction was in an old, industrial part of town, with a few vacant and derelict buildings. There was a chain-link fence all the way along the tracks.

She stopped the car and got out. The tracks were a few yards away, and she could hear the trains in the distance, a faint background noise.

The tracks were deserted, and the landscape was flat and open. She could see the junction up ahead. There was nobody lying there. Nobody she could see at all.

How about those buildings?

Caitlin went and checked each one, but the doors were firmly locked from the outside, with rusted locks.

That left only one option, and it was the other set of tracks. The other junction.

Caitlin quickly texted Nathan, telling him what she'd done and where she was going, sending through the coordinates of the final, remaining junction.

Then she hurried back to her car and made her way to the next set of tracks. The junction she needed was just a few miles away. In fact, the same road, curving through the industrial part of the town, crossed the tracks twice at different ends of town.

This area, as she approached it, looked to be even more forlorn. The junction was a joining place between old, rusted rails and new, shiny ones.

Caitlin got out of the car, striding over an empty parking lot, where the concrete was cracked, shattered, and strewn with weeds. She marched down the old tracks themselves, looking around first hopefully and then anxiously, her confidence in her theory weakening with every step. She couldn't see the killer or anyone on the tracks. The area was completely clear.

She was about to leave when she saw that ahead of her, half hidden by an outcrop of bushes, was an old, abandoned boxcar.

Suddenly, what Malcolm Coombes had told them resonated in her head. He'd said he had been locked away somewhere dark, lying against a steel wall while he was interrogated.

That sounded a lot like what she was seeing here. Was it possible this was where the victims were kept when they were questioned?

Her heart in her mouth, Caitlin moved closer.

And, as she approached, she heard a sound from inside that chilled her blood.

It was a woman's voice, and she was pleading. Pleading for her life.

"You don't understand," she was saying tearfully. "I'm leaving to save myself."

"I don't care," the voice came back harshly. "Why should I care why you decide to do anything? Doing it will doom you!"

"Well, if I stay, my life's destroyed too. You try living with an abusive narcissist for five years!"

The words resounded in Caitlin's head as she rushed around the boxcar, desperate to find the gap or entrance that would allow her in. This was an emergency situation. The woman he'd abducted was about to leave an abuser. And this evil killer didn't care. He was working himself up to kill her regardless. Because in the end, this was all about the kill for him. It always had been.

There was the door, halfway along the opposite side. Closed.

Caitlin could hear shouting from within the boxcar. She could hear the killer yelling, and she could hear the woman crying. She flung herself against the door, trying to open it, but it was jammed and would not budge.

There was a sudden silence from inside, and she knew that they knew she was there. Most probably, he had left her and rushed to the door, ready for what might happen next.

She'd be going into an ambush for sure, and she'd need to be ready to fight from the moment she broke through.

She took out her gun and held it firmly. With all her strength, taking a run at it this time, she hurled herself shoulder first into the door.

The door gave way, and she stumbled in. It was utterly dark inside. Total, disorienting blackness met her gaze. Where the hell was he? Left? Right? Nobody was saying a word, and she could hear no sound.

Then, suddenly, a flashlight shone at her, blinding her. Behind her, the door slammed shut, leaving that beam of light as the only, blinding source. She flinched away from it, swinging the gun in that direction, but a hand grabbed her wrist and wrenched it sideways. He was going to grab her gun, she realized, and then it would be over.

Caitlin tried to grasp his wrist, but he wrenched it away, and the next moment, she flinched aside as a whistling blow came down.

He'd almost gotten to her. Almost hurt her bad. She couldn't risk shooting in this darkness because she had no idea where the victim was.

And she couldn't risk him getting her gun, and he was going to. Caitlin thought fast. With a pang of regret, she did the only thing she could. She dropped the gun and kicked it away, hearing his grunt of anger.

Now it was him and her, in a hand-to-hand fight that Caitlin knew was going to turn deadly.

CHAPTER THIRTY

In the almost total darkness of the abandoned boxcar, Caitlin found herself fighting for her life. This psychopath, Tony Lang, was on the attack. Her feet slipped on the cold, steel floor as she tried to get her footing, to group herself for the fight.

He was stronger than she'd anticipated. Faster too. And he held the flashlight, a blinding weapon of light.

In the darkness, she lashed out at him, but he evaded her grasp and grabbed her instead. His fingers bit into her arm, hard, and Caitlin twisted away with a gasp, retreating a few steps into the dark, gloomy space.

Gasping, her heart pounding, she took stock of her surroundings. This boxcar was about fifty feet long, and probably nine feet wide. The door where she'd come through was in the middle point of the wall. All the way at the far end behind her, she glimpsed his victim, a dark shape on the floor. There was a large pile of sacking and rags in that corner, which he must have stashed there previously to wrap his victims. The woman was pressed up against it now.

She couldn't let him get to her. If he did, then he would have a huge advantage. He'd be able to force her away by threatening to kill this woman, or he could even use her as a shield.

Right now, he was facing the woman, Laverne Mills. She was closer, with her back to this victim. Her gun was somewhere behind her—and that was another reason for not retreating. She couldn't see where it was. He might be able to and might try to force her in that direction so he could grab it.

Now, Caitlin and Tony were sizing each other up, preparing to fight, like two boxers in a ring.

He lunged forward, shockingly fast, and Caitlin twisted aside, kicking out as she evaded him. The blow landed on his knee, but it wasn't hard enough, he was already turning sideways to avoid it before lashing at her again with a hammer blow of his fist. She tried to dodge it, but she had underestimated his reach, and it caught her a glancing punch on the arm that almost knocked her flying with its power.

Caitlin gasped, hearing him laugh. This was bad. Because he'd gotten an advantage, he'd gotten confidence. He had the ascendancy now, and she could see him starting to realize that she was not as dangerous an adversary as he'd first thought.

"You a cop?" he said, his voice hard and mocking. "You fight like a cop. Pathetic. Like you learned how from a book."

She lunged for him, but he sidestepped her and grabbed her arm again, holding her in a painful grip.

"You can't stop me!" he hissed into her ear. "You're going to end up like her. Out on the tracks. You made a bad decision coming here. The wrong one. I can already see that."

"Let go!" she gasped, lashing out at him, but he evaded her again, and this time, he managed to grab her wrist. He pulled her to him and then twisted her arm up behind her back.

Caitlin gritted her teeth, feeling the flare of agony that she knew would quickly incapacitate her. But just because he had the advantage didn't mean she was out of the fight. She stamped down hard with her heel, got him on his ankle, and unbalanced him enough to wrench herself away. As she did that, he dropped the flashlight. Seeing her chance, Caitlin reacted, lightning fast.

Quickly, just like she'd done with the gun, she kicked the light out of reach. Now, the boxcar was dimly lit, with giant shadows looming each time one of them moved, but at least he couldn't use it to blind her.

He was furious. She heard his indrawn hiss of rage.

And then he stopped playing around. Now, she thought that was what he'd been doing. The fun was over. He came at her again, and this time, he wasn't trying to fool around. He was deadly serious, and she knew that he was going to kill her.

He caught her a flash of a second before she realized he was about to. She tried to twist away, but it was too late. He struck her, a ringing blow with the back of his hand that sent her sprawling across the floor. The metal slammed into her arms and her shoulders as she tried to roll with the blow.

Frantically, feeling battered and bruised, she scrambled to her feet as fast as she could, fast enough to kick out and get him squarely in the thigh as he tried to get past her. She'd hoped to get him in the groin, but in the darkness and in her haste, her aim was off. Even so, it was enough to throw him off balance and slow him down—for the moment she needed to get her own balance again.

As she tried to get her breath back, she saw his shadow looming over her and then he kicked her, hard. He'd been aiming for her knee, but managing to twist away in time, she took the blow on her lower thigh. The pain flared, and she gasped, trying to avoid the next kick, stumbling over a ridge on the floor.

She ducked, but it caught her on the shoulder, and that was enough for him to grab her again, and this time, to press her face down against the steel floor and hold her there. His hands were crushing her. He was so strong that she couldn't get up. He must weigh 250 pounds at least. Heavy, bulky, and murderous. She had to do something, because she was moments away from being potentially disabled, knocked out, or even killed and then he could do what he wanted with his other victim.

"I'm going to enjoy killing you," he whispered into her ear, his voice full of triumph. It sent a dark wave of fear through her, and she tried her best to fight against it. Her voice was the only weapon she still had for the moment. Her cheek was crushed against the frigid metal, but she could still speak.

"That's what it's all about for you, isn't it? The kill? You're doing this because you enjoy it, right?"

He paused, hesitating, as if shocked by what she'd said. "I do it because I have to. I have to save people from their choices."

"That's all that matters to you, is it? Saving them?"

"Yes. That's all that matters. Saving them and killing the ones who aren't making the right choice. The safe choice."

"But then you're a killer. You're a murderer. You're not saving anyone," Caitlin pointed out, but while she was speaking, she was looking for a weak point. If she couldn't throw him off balance physically, she needed to try and do it mentally. And then, perhaps, she'd get the chance to gain the edge in their combat again.

"I'm a hero," he said, and his voice was so cold that it chilled her. She knew this man had been through hell, that he'd lost his entire family in a freak accident, but she had the strong feeling that he'd been a psychopath long before that had happened. It had simply been the catalyst for him to begin, and if it hadn't been that, then it might have been something else.

"You're nothing more than a deluded freak show!" she shouted, wanting to anger him into action, even though it was getting harder to speak and harder to breathe with his weight on her, not to mention the pain. This was terrifying. This man was truly deranged, he could kill her in a moment, and the only reason he hadn't was that the argument had sidetracked him, and he wanted to win it.

"I'm not crazy!" he screamed. "Your words are just hot air! It doesn't mean anything! You can't stop me!" he shouted, and now his voice was triumphant.

But as he shouted those words, he was off balance. He took a fraction of the weight off her, and she was able to twist away from him slightly. He clawed at her, but she was already moving, writhing out of his grasp, springing to her feet. She backed away.

With an angry cry, he did what she'd known he would do.

He attacked.

Caitlin watched him move, the computer in her mind replaying every combat session she'd been in, every street fight she'd been part of during breathless, bloody, dangerous takedowns. She could see one opening, just one more chance to take him down.

It was nothing more than a split-second opportunity, and she knew she had to seize it or die.

CHAPTER THIRTY ONE

As Tony Lang launched himself at her in the gloom of the boxcar, his arms reaching for her, fingers so powerful they were like giant, steel hooks, Caitlin put her final, desperate plan into action.

It was as risky as hell, and one small slip, one miscalculation, would see her dead in a moment. But she had no other choice.

Drawing in a breath, tensing her muscles, she ducked down and to one side, before he could grab her again.

And then, with what felt like a superhuman effort, she hurled herself forward, at him, aiming low, going for his knees, needing to knock him completely off balance to get him down on the floor.

She didn't have time to think about the fact that he outweighed her by well over a hundred pounds. She only had time to think that if she tackled him with enough force, then she'd get the advantage.

She connected. He stumbled, lost his footing, and with a cry of rage and frustration, he fell backwards.

As they fell in a tumble of arms and legs, she fell on top of him.

He tried to pull her off, tried to get her into a choke hold, but she shoved her knee into his solar plexus, and now he was the one choking as the air whooshed out of him in a violent cough. She had his hands, flung all her weight against them, but he was still struggling with everything he had. He was gasping, fighting for breath.

"Bitch," he panted, in a crazed voice that was almost inhuman. "You're going to be sorry you ever messed with me."

She hit him again, and he caught her fist in a tight grip.

"You're the one who'll be sorry," she said, wrenching her hand away, and this time, finally, she managed to get a grip on his neck. If she had to cut his air off, get him unconscious to be able to handcuff him, that was what she would do. It might be the only way she could. But he was yelling now, thrashing wildly, clearly in a panic now that the tables had turned, and he was the one in her power.

As he fought back ferociously, using his brutal strength to try and twist himself out of her grasp, she knew that this attempt was going to take everything out of her, and she wasn't even sure if she could do it.

He was so powerful and determined that she felt as if her grip was slipping away with every second that passed.

She tightened her hold and tried to stay calm, using her mind to focus her strength and her determination to take him down. Yes, he was struggling, but his main aim was to loosen her grip on his throat. That gave her the chance to grab his wrist, and if she could hold him for long enough that she could get the cuff on, she'd be halfway there.

She gritted her teeth and pushed her weight into him, feeling her muscles straining as she attempted to keep him in place. She had to keep going, no matter what, to fight him down until he was cuffed and unable to move. But Lang moved, twisted, and the next moment, in a vicious whiplash, he tore Caitlin's hand from his throat.

Adrenaline flared inside her. This was going to go so bad, so fast. She lunged for his wrist and managed to cling onto it, holding him at bay before he could grab hold of her. That had been his intention. Her arm quivered with the strain of holding him.

"You're not going to do it," he hissed. "I'm going to get away. You're too weak for this. I'm going to get out of here after killing both of you, and nobody will find me again."

As he wrenched his wrist out of her grasp and his hand battered against her, that threat felt all too real to her. Her head snapped back as he bludgeoned her, and she felt her teeth crunch together painfully. But she managed to ride the blow partway so it didn't do the damage he intended. He hissed in anger.

She got hold of his arm again, even though her eyes were watering from the impact, and dug her fingers into his flesh, shoving down harder, using her entire body weight to keep him pinned in place. Her muscles screamed in protest, but she kept going, determined to take him down.

He writhed away from her, trying to twist free, and she narrowly missed a violent headbutt that would have crushed her nose. Jerking back, she saw an opening, a chance to claw back the advantage if she acted quickly. She ducked, letting his arm go past her and then grabbed his other wrist in a vice grip. She twisted and pulled, managing to wrench his hand back and around, her fingers digging deep into his skin as she managed to get one of the cuffs around his wrist.

But he was fighting even harder now, his muscles bunching as he tried to get away. A lucky kick caught her square on the shin, sending a flash of pain through her leg.

She gasped, feeling the force of the impact, and her grip loosened slightly. He took the opportunity to wrench himself away, nearly yanking his arm right out of her grasp.

Caitlin's heart pounded in her chest as she scrambled to get back into the fight. She had almost had him, but now she'd completely lost the advantage.

She gritted her teeth and lunged forward, getting hold of his arm again. She twisted and pulled, using her entire body weight to try and force his arm back so that she could fasten the other handcuff.

But she knew her strength was running out. She'd given all she could in this battle with a far stronger adversary. If she wasn't able to fasten the cuff this time, then the opportunity would be gone forever, and she would have lost not only her criminal, but her own life, and Laverne's as well.

Caitlin lunged with the handcuff. But his arm slipped out of her grasp, causing her to gasp in frustration.

Her chance was gone, her strength was ebbing, and this criminal was refusing to give in.

With a flash of fear, she realized this meant it was over. She'd reached her limits, and any moment now, he was going to break free and escape.

CHAPTER THIRTY TWO

The very next moment, the door of the boxcar burst open, letting in what felt to Caitlin like a blaze of daylight in the near darkness.

There was Nathan, standing in the doorway, gun drawn. He took one shocked look at the scene, at Caitlin wrestling with the killer, and he rushed over.

Lang was on the point of breaking free. He cried out in surprise as Nathan grabbed his wrist from behind, wrenching his hand into the air, grabbing the cuff that was swinging from it. And then, with Caitlin holding the man down with the last of her remaining strength, Nathan got the other arm into the cuff.

"No, you don't! You can't do this!" Lang bellowed in furious tones. "This wasn't supposed to happen. This wasn't in my plan! I won't go down."

"You can and will," Nathan said, moving aside to dodge another vicious kick. "You're under arrest now, and there are more police outside. This is it for you. It's over."

His words, and the threatening tone, finally seemed to subdue Lang's aggression. His struggles lessened, and he glanced suspiciously at the door.

Caitlin was gasping for breath. She felt utterly spent, as if this fight had taken everything out of her. But they'd got him. They'd got the killer, and Nathan hadn't been bluffing. More police were on the scene. She heard footsteps outside, the crackle of radios.

Two officers burst into the boxcar, and behind them, a paramedic rushed in. The beams of flashlights further cut the darkness. Voices resounded inside the metal shell.

Caitlin scrambled to her feet.

"I'm okay," she gasped to the paramedic who was approaching her anxiously. "Help her, first. Help Laverne."

She rushed with him to the victim, feeling a huge sense of relief to see that Laverne's eyes were open, and she seemed unhurt, apart from a graze on her temple.

"I was watching the fight," she whispered to Caitlin. "Thank you for saving me."

Caitlin bent down and squeezed her hand, which felt cold and weak. "I'm glad I could," she whispered back, emotion rushing through her that this woman would still have the opportunity to recover, to restart her life, and hopefully still have time to escape the abusive relationship she'd been trapped in.

She'd still be able to make the decision that would save her, despite the psychotic man who'd been intent on ripping her life away forever.

And then, feeling relieved beyond measure, she turned back to Nathan, who had been supervising as Lang, securely handcuffed, was led out in the direction of a police van. He was bellowing in rage, as if ready to fight all over again. Most likely, this badly damaged and psychotic man would spend the rest of his life in a secure psychiatric ward.

"Boy, was I glad to see you," she said to Nathan. "If you hadn't have gotten here when you did, I don't know if I could have held him. I was trying, but I was all the way at my limits."

"It felt like touch and go while I was on the way. I'm impressed you managed to hold him for so long. I couldn't believe how strong he was."

It had taken every technique she knew, and all of her own strength, to stop him. Her muscles were telling her so. But there had been everything to lose.

Now that the place was abuzz with police and the arrest was made, they could talk for a minute.

"He was furious, and he threatened that he was going to escape and disappear after killing us both." Caitlin felt cold at what that would have meant.

"I wish I'd been with you. I thought I was getting somewhere with the psychologist," Nathan said. "Eventually, he cracked and confessed, it turned out he'd been seeing some patients 'off the record' after hours and conducting affairs with them at the same time. Highly unethical, and why he was refusing to talk."

"Definitely a crime, but not the crime we wanted," Caitlin agreed. "If he'd been honest about it, we'd have arrived here even sooner."

"How did you work it out?"

"It was the junctions and Tony Lang's background. I worked out that he was choosing junctions that were close to road crossings. Using them to show the consequences of what he thought were bad choices, because in his mind, his own choice had been bad when his family were killed at a crossing." She shivered hard.

"When I saw your text, I thought that this has to be the place. I called the backup immediately. I thought every moment might count." He cleared his throat, looking sternly at her. "Caitlin, do you think it was the right thing to go in there alone? That was incredibly dangerous."

She shrugged, although she felt a nervous defensiveness inside her that this might lead to history repeating itself. "I had no choice. I had to do what I could and get there as fast as possible. I did try to call."

"Yeah," Nathan shrugged. "True. Next time, when you go out on your own, I'm going to keep my phone open and not have it on silent."

And that was it. Caitlin felt a sense of utter relief that her partner understood and supported her decision. It made her feel that this task force was where she belonged.

"Oh, I'd better call Aniyah," Caitlin said. "She's going to need to speak to the senator and tell him that we've been working around the clock, following strong leads—and that it all worked out and the killer is caught!"

EPILOGUE

Four days later, Caitlin had not expected to find herself back in Atlanta again, but here she was, on a flying visit with a mission in mind.

Two days ago, she'd contacted the storage company who'd been stowing a few of her boxes for her. Having been transferred to different FBI offices a few times over the past years, she hadn't wanted to unpack everything in her shoebox-sized Atlanta apartment.

Now that she was confident that she'd be based in Kansas City for a while, and there was more space in her new place, she'd decided to go through the boxes on site at the storage facility, throw away or donate what she didn't need, and ship what she did.

It would also be a chance to visit Mike, and Caitlin was going to make it a surprise. They'd spoken a couple of times that week, and their conversations had been friendly and flirtatious, and he'd told her he really was keen to make the move and just needed more time.

She'd made sure that he wasn't working this afternoon, without telling him why. She had brought a bottle of champagne with her and planned to arrive at his place with it and take him to dinner. Then, tomorrow morning, she'd go through the boxes and then fly back to Kansas City.

It was late afternoon, and Caitlin felt hopeful and excited as she climbed the stairs to Mike's apartment, which was a couple of streets away from the school where he worked.

She was sure he'd be interested to hear about the adventures she'd had on her recent case, and especially the follow up she'd heard today—that Laverne was now safely out of Ohio. She'd made it into her new life, left her husband for good, and Caitlin hoped that her future would be safe and happy.

With future on her own mind, she wanted this visit to cement things between herself and Mike, and also to be a chance to speak face to face with him and find out if he really wanted their relationship to get closer in the short term. If he didn't, then they'd have to agree to the "long distance" relationship that she didn't really want. Would she settle for it?

She guessed that depended on his long-term goals, as well as hers. But without discussion, they could get no further. Excited by the thought of the surprise, she was wearing a pair of new jeans, a figure-hugging black top that she knew suited her, and she'd even put on make-up, a rare occurrence.

Walking up to his door, she tapped on it, smiling to herself as she hid the champagne behind her back. She heard footsteps, and the door opened.

Caitlin, to her shock, found herself staring into the wide, blue eyes of a petite, curvaceous blonde who looked to be in her mid-twenties.

For a horrified moment, she simply stared at her, taking this in while her mind raced.

"Who are you?" she blurted out.

"I … I'm Leanne. I thought you were Mike, coming home. I was waiting here for him."

"Why?" Caitlin asked, although she felt her world was falling apart, and it was very clear why, wearing a revealing top and enough perfume to sink a ship, this woman was inside Mike's apartment.

"I … er … we're good friends. A recent friendship," the woman admitted, blushing in an attractive way. "But who are you? A neighbor? Were you looking for him?" Clearly not the quickest on the uptake, she frowned in a puzzled way.

Caitlin was feeling sick inside. "You're dating?" she asked.

"I—we're dating, I guess."

"Since when?" Caitlin asked, feeling the pain in her chest like a knife.

"We met at the school, about two weeks ago, and hit it off. But seriously, who are you?" she asked, now sounding curious and looking worried.

Shock was still resounding through Caitlin, but now fury was overtaking it. She was not going to show this woman how upset she was that her boyfriend had just outed himself as a total cheater. Not when there were better ways to do it.

"I'm his previous girlfriend," Caitlin said, trying to get the right note of fake honey into her voice. "Mike and I broke up very recently. In fact, we broke up just thirty seconds ago. So, our relationships with him did overlap, I'm sorry to tell you," she said cheerily, seeing the woman's now aghast face. "I dropped by to say goodbye to him and brought this. Be sure to give it to him, won't you?"

She thrust the champagne bottle into the girl's surprised hands and turned on her heel, striding away before this new girlfriend had the chance to speak another word.

Red hot anger consumed her as she stormed the whole way down the stairs and out to her rental car, which she started up with a roar. She was done with Mike. Done! She now regretted every single moment she'd ever spent with him, every nice thing she'd ever done for him. No tender memories here, Caitlin fumed, speeding away from his apartment and heading for the storage facility. Not one shred of sympathy remained. She never wanted to think again about that lying cheat, or was he more of a cheating liar, she wondered angrily as she drove.

It felt like every man she'd trusted in Atlanta was out to get her, she decided darkly, remembering the unethical behavior of her partner, Fitch, and her boss, Hume, at the FBI offices, and the way they'd forced her out.

Now, Mike had added himself to the list of backstabbers.

It was a ten-minute drive to the storage facility, and Caitlin did it in seven, seething every yard of the way.

At least she'd gotten here an hour before it closed. She could go through the boxes now, go straight to the airport, and fly back tonight.

She rushed in and headed straight for her unit. She unlocked the door and stared at the three large, cardboard boxes that were stacked there. Using the edge of her key, she cut through the tape of the first one and opened it.

Old books galore in here, some dating from many years back. These, she could donate. She'd read them, so they might as well go to a good cause and let others enjoy them. But as she was sifting through the pile, in case there were one or two she couldn't bear to part with, she saw something that wasn't a novel.

Lifting it out, Caitlin stared in surprise at it. It was a diary, but it was not hers.

This was Ella's diary. She blinked in shock as the memories rushed back.

Caitlin knew she'd kept a diary, but she never knew what had happened to it. Somehow, it had ended up here in this stash of books.

And a diary might point the way to how she'd disappeared. What if there had been something happening in her life? This could be an important clue.

Quickly, Caitlin checked the entries, paging hurriedly through. This diary was detailed. Ella had poured out her thoughts and feelings on the pages. This was a treasure trove of information. Her heart raced as she saw that the last entry had been made the morning that Ella had left home and boarded that train.

Her eyes caught on one phrase in the closely scribbled page.

"And I can't wait to get away from D. Just in time, if I'm lucky," she'd written.

D? Who was D? Did he have anything to do with her abduction? This sounded like serious trouble, something that Caitlin had never known about.

Now, she was going to find out.

COME TAKE ME
(A Caitlin Dare FBI Suspense Thriller—Book 3)

When a new serial killer strikes, abducting victims from lonely train stations across the country, FBI Special Agent Caitlin Dare, teaming up with the rail police, must race to crack his mysterious M.O. Why is he targeting train stations? Where is he taking them? And could Caitlin herself be next?

"Molly Black has written a taut thriller that will keep you on the edge of your seat… I absolutely loved this book and can't wait to read the next book in the series!"
—Reader review for Girl One: Murder

COME TAKE ME is book #3 of a brand-new series by critically acclaimed and #1 bestselling mystery and suspense author Molly Black, whose books have received over 2,000 five-star reviews and ratings.

The FBI is alarmed by the rash of killings on trains throughout the country, and they realize they have to put together a joint task force to tackle it. Through a partnership with the rail police, FBI Special Agent Cailtin Dare is chosen to spearhead the new unit designed to hunt killers using trains across the country.

But Cailtin remains haunted by memories of her missing sister, her unsolved case, her erratic conductor uncle, and a harrowing fear of trains.

The tension with Caitlin's new partner doesn't help, either.

Can Caitlin keep her own demons at bay long enough to face her past—and catch a killer?

A page-turning and harrowing crime thriller featuring a brilliant and tortured FBI agent, the Caitlin Dare series is a riveting mystery, packed with non-stop action, suspense, twists and turns, revelations, and driven by a breakneck pace that will keep you flipping pages late into the night. Fans of Rachel Caine, Teresa Driscoll and Robert Dugoni are sure to fall in love.

Future books in the series are also available.

"I binge read this book. It hooked me in and didn't stop till the last few pages… I look forward to reading more!"
—Reader review for Found You

"I loved this book! Fast-paced plot, great characters and interesting insights into investigating cold cases. I can't wait to read the next book!"
—Reader review for Girl One: Murder

"Very good book… You will feel like you are right there looking for the kidnapper! I know I will be reading more in this series!"
—Reader review for Girl One: Murder

"This is a very well written book and holds your interest from page 1… Definitely looking forward to reading the next one in the series, and hopefully others as well!"
—Reader review for Girl One: Murder

"Wow, I cannot wait for the next in this series. Starts with a bang and just keeps going."
—Reader review for Girl One: Murder

"Well written book with a great plot, one that will keep you up at night. A page turner!"
—Reader review for Girl One: Murder

"Sooo soo good! There are a few unforeseen twists… I binge read this like I binge watch Netflix. It just sucks you in."
—Reader review for Found You

Molly Black

Bestselling author Molly Black is author of the MAYA GRAY FBI suspense thriller series, comprising nine books (and counting); of the RYLIE WOLF FBI suspense thriller series, comprising six books; of the TAYLOR SAGE FBI suspense thriller series, comprising eight books; of the KATIE WINTER FBI suspense thriller series, comprising eleven books (and counting); of the RUBY HUNTER FBI suspense thriller series, comprising five books (and counting); of the CAITLIN DARE FBI suspense thriller series, comprising five books (and counting); and of the REESE LINK mystery series, comprising five books (and counting).

An avid reader and lifelong fan of the mystery and thriller genres, Molly loves to hear from you, so please feel free to visit www.mollyblackauthor.com to learn more and stay in touch.

BOOKS BY MOLLY BLACK

MAYA GRAY MYSTERY SERIES
GIRL ONE: MURDER (Book #1)
GIRL TWO: TAKEN (Book #2)
GIRL THREE: TRAPPED (Book #3)
GIRL FOUR: LURED (Book #4)
GIRL FIVE: BOUND (Book #5)
GIRL SIX: FORSAKEN (Book #6)
GIRL SEVEN: CRAVED (Book #7)
GIRL EIGHT: HUNTED (Book #8)
GIRL NINE: GONE (Book #9)

RYLIE WOLF FBI SUSPENSE THRILLER
FOUND YOU (Book #1)
CAUGHT YOU (Book #2)
SEE YOU (Book #3)
WANT YOU (Book #4)
TAKE YOU (Book #5)
DARE YOU (Book #6)

TAYLOR SAGE FBI SUSPENSE THRILLER
DON'T LOOK (Book #1)
DON'T BREATHE (Book #2)
DON'T RUN (Book #3)
DON'T FLINCH (Book #4)
DON'T REMEMBER (Book #5)
DON'T TELL (Book #6)

KATIE WINTER FBI SUSPENSE THRILLER
SAVE ME (Book #1)
REACH ME (Book #2)
HIDE ME (Book #3)
BELIEVE ME (Book #4)

HELP ME (Book #5)
FORGET ME (Book #6)
HOLD ME (Book #7)
PROTECT ME (Book #8)
REMEMBER ME (Book #9)
CATCH ME (Book #10)
WATCH ME (Book #11)

RUBY HUNTER FBI SUSPENSE THRILLER
IF I RUN (Book #1)
IF I TELL (Book #2)
IF I LIVE (Book #3)
IF I FORGET (Book #4)
IF I RETURN (Book #5)

CAITLIN DARE FBI SUSPENSE THRILLER
COME GET ME (Book #1)
COME FIND ME (Book #2)
COME TAKE ME (Book #3)
COME CATCH ME (Book #4)
COME SAVE ME (Book #5)

REESE LINK MYSTERY
BEYOND REASON (Book #1)
BEYOND REACH (Book #2)
BEYOND REPAIR (Book #3)
BEYOND DOUBT (Book #4)
BEYOND NORMAL (Book #5)

Made in the USA
Monee, IL
23 May 2025